"We Can Set t[...]
Commercial U[...]

Trent said. "We're coming back from a party and you say something like 'Weren't you spending a bit too much time with that redhead?' See, you're jealous and—"

Lily jumped right in. "Why should I be jealous? Why should I care if you were talking to some flashy redhead?"

"Because you're supposed to be married to me."

"If I were," Lily answered angrily, "you could talk to anyone you liked. I'm not the jealous type."

"I'll remember that," Trent said lightly, but there seemed to Lily to be something more behind his words.

CASSANDRA BISHOP

traces her love of romance to an adolescence spent reading and rereading *Gone with the Wind*. But before she became a romance writer she tried several careers, including working in an art gallery. Now, with the full support of her husband, she spends her days writing stories of dreams come true.

Dear Reader,

Thank you so much for all the letters I have received praising our SILHOUETTE DESIRE series. All your comments have proved invaluable to us, as we strive to publish the best in contemporary romance.

DESIREs feature all of the elements you like to see in a romance, plus a more sensual, provocative story. So if you want to experience all the excitement, passion and joy of falling in love, then SILHOUETTE DESIRE is for you.

I hope you enjoy this book and all the wonderful stories to come from SILHOUETTE DESIRE. If you have any thoughts you'd like to share with us on SILHOUETTE DESIRE, then please write to me at the address below:

Jane Nicholls
Silhouette Books
PO Box 177
Dunton Green
Sevenoaks
Kent
TN13 2YE

CASSANDRA BISHOP

Madison Avenue Marriage

Silhouette Desire

Published by Silhouette Books

Copyright © 1984 by Cassandra Bishop

First printing 1984

British Library C.I.P.

Bishop, Cassandra
    Madison Avenue marriage.—(Silhouette desire)
    I. Title
    813'.54[F]   PS3552.I759/

    ISBN 0 340 36164 6

Printed and bound in Great Britain for
Hodder and Stoughton Paperbacks, a
division of Hodder and Stoughton Ltd.,
Mill Road, Dunton Green, Sevenoaks,
Kent (Editorial Office: 47 Bedford
Square, London, WC1 3DP) by
Richard Clay (The Chaucer Press) Ltd.,
Bungay, Suffolk

Madison Avenue Marriage

1

Lily Lansden stood on the platform, watching the train from which she'd just disembarked disappear amidst swirls of snow, and cursed herself. When she had boarded the train at Grand Central Station, in New York City, the sky had been a clear, brilliant blue. Now she was in Connecticut, and it was snowing. Soft flakes settled on her straight blond hair like frozen goose down. The temperature was hovering, she guessed, in the mid-twenties, so at least the sable she wore was appropriate, but her high heels were completely wrong for the weather, and her legs, clad only in the sheerest of silk stockings, were beginning to feel frostbitten. Snow covered the tips of her expensive green suede pumps as Lily shifted her feet anxiously, wincing as miniature mountains of snow avalanched off the tips of her toes, leaving wet patches that she knew would harden and crack when the suede dried.

She gripped her suitcase tensely in her ungloved hand. Inside were several books and a few clothes, including a pair of jeans and some boots. But of course there was no place to change, so they were useless. The rest of her "wardrobe" had been chosen for her, and would be coming up later in the day with her agent. If her ride didn't come soon, she realized, he'd find her frozen to the platform. She imagined the headline: "Famous Writer Found Frozen to Death in Danbury/If Only She'd Worn the Right Clothes!"

She squinted her bright blue eyes and searched the

road in front of her, though really she was searching for the road itself, because she could barely see two feet ahead.

"When I see that man . . ." Lily's hands rose in a throttling gesture, when suddenly someone loomed out of the snow and jiggled her elbow. Lily gasped in surprise, and then, thinking quickly, realized exactly who it had to be.

"Excuse me," the stranger said. "Are you—"

"Yes, I am," Lily responded impatiently, not even allowing him to complete his sentence. "I'm Lily Lansden, and you're late."

"No I'm not, I'm Lawrence," he replied. "And you're waiting in the wrong place. You were supposed to be in front of the station house door, not lolling around on the platform."

"I'm not lolling, I'm being buried alive in snow. And no one ever said anything about a door. I think you . . ." But Lily's sentence trailed off. She had finally raised her eyes to meet his, and she was confronted with the most beautiful pair of eyes she had ever seen in her life. They were purple. Of all the colors in the world for a man's eyes to be, they were a most inappropriate deep purple, like a bed of spring violets. They ran the risk of making him effeminate, but as Lily's eyes took in the rest of him she could see that they most definitely had the opposite effect. He was all man, from the top of his straight black hair to his long lanky legs clad in a pair of black leather riding boots. Spiky lashes surrounded his extraordinarily large eyes, and his wide, angular cheekbones pointed straight at them, making them even more noticeable than his generous, full-lipped mouth. He was so gorgeous that she wanted to pinch him to make sure he was real. So this was the man her agent had chosen to be her husband. Not bad at all!

She stopped her examination long enough to finish her sentence. "And I think you're rude."

He glanced at her skeptically. "And I think you're

harebrained to be standing here in the snow wearing high heels and stockings. Don't you know how to dress for this kind of weather?"

Lily's temper flared. If there was one thing she knew she wasn't, it was harebrained. "For your information, Mr.—" She stopped abruptly. No one had bothered to tell her what his real name was.

"Mr. Daily. Trent Daily. But perhaps you should get used to my new name. Lawrence Lansden." He gave her a mocking smile, the kind of ironic grin that would get any woman's back up, especially when it came from a man as handsome as Trent Daily was.

"Yes, that's right, but I think I'll call you Trent." Lily paused for emphasis. "Until I *have* to call you Lawrence."

"That's fine, Lily, whatever you wish. But do you think we could postpone this fascinating battle of wits until we get ourselves into my car? It's too cold out here." Trent Daily offered his arm like the gentleman Lily was already sure he wasn't. "Would you like some assistance? Can I take your bag?" he said mockingly, wearing the overly solicitous face of a bellboy.

"No, thank you." Lily shrugged off his hand at her elbow. "I can make it on my own."

"As you please," Trent replied, and began to stride quickly down the platform while Lily, with small, clumsy steps, tried to keep up with his pace. He was walking quickly, she was sure, just to embarrass her, to make her feel clumsy and helpless since, she was *also* sure, he was used to women following him wherever he went. She'd have to let him know, and soon, that she hadn't gotten to be a mystery writer who was translated into seventeen foreign languages and enjoyed the world over by being a meek little lady who followed in a man's wake.

A building loomed up before them, dingy brown in the gray and white snow that swirled around it. Trent walked around to the front and stopped by the door, under an overhang.

"Now, this is where you were supposed to be." He pulled her under the overhang. "Waiting at this door. See?" He pointed at the bare ground beneath their feet. "No snow. You would have been protected from the storm, with the wind at your back. You wouldn't have ruined those pretty shoes." His mood suddenly changed from reprimanding to playful as he pulled her closer and wrapped his arm around her waist. "I don't want my wife catching cold, you know."

Lily was at a loss for what to do. As she stood beneath the overhang, wrapped in Trent's arm, protected from the snowflakes whose sharp edges had bitten into the tender skin of her cheeks just a moment ago, she felt a sudden, unreasonable and completely unexpected thrill of excitement. Trent's touch had an effect on her that was difficult to ignore.

"And now," he said, chucking her under the chin and pulling her face up toward his, "may I kiss the bride?"

Before she even had a chance to protest, he kissed her confidently, as if there were no reason in the world for her to deny him. His mouth tasted of coffee, and Lily had always loved coffee. But she didn't love Trent Daily. . . . She didn't even know him! His body was warm and inviting against hers, and she was so cold that she instinctively pulled him closer, then furiously pushed him away, using her suitcase as a barrier between them. What did he think he was doing?

"Listen, Trent." Lily's breath steamed in the frigid air. "I think we'd better get something straight right now." She stood there shivering, half from the cold and half from anger. "You are not my husband. You're hired help. I suggest you act accordingly."

He straightened his back, clicked his heels together, saluted and barked, "Yes, ma'am!"

"That's not what I meant, and you know it!"

"What do you mean . . . darling?" His eyes sparkled like amethysts.

"Don't call me that!"

"What should I call you? Lily love? Yes, I'll call you Lily love; I like that." He was relentless.

"You'll call me Lily and nothing else. And furthermore"—her anger had given her a clear mind—"in front of people you'll act like my husband, but when there's no audience to watch you you're just Joe Blow from Kokomo as far as I'm concerned."

"But what about as far as *I'm* concerned? Maybe I don't think I'm Joe Blow from Kokomo."

"I doubt you do. You probably think you're the Sheik of Araby. . . . But I don't care what you think." Lily switched gears, hoping that reason would appeal to him. "Look, Trent. My agent hired you because I don't have a husband." Trent looked like he was about to burst into laughter. *"At the moment,"* she finished firmly, although she half wanted to laugh herself. Now that Trent, or rather Lawrence Lansden, was standing in front of her in the flesh, she was suddenly hit by the absurdity of her situation. He must think her a pathetic creature, having to hire a husband. No wonder he was laughing at her. But Lily had made the decision to go through with this crazy scheme, and once she made up her mind she always followed through, no matter what. Yes, she wanted to laugh too. She wanted to laugh to keep from crying.

"Listen, Trent, or Lawrence, or whatever you're called, we're going up to this house in Litchfield to shoot a commercial for Albert Fountaine's winery. We're going to sip champagne for him and do whatever else it is we have to do, and we'll both make an enormous amount of money. This is a business deal. Let's keep it that way." To close the matter, she changed the subject. "Now, where's the car? I'm freezing."

Trent folded his arms across his chest and smiled a knowing, superior smile. "You're getting awfully angry over just a simple kiss."

She fought back. "It *was* simple. Simple and dull."

Trent laughed out loud. "All right, Lily. You win the first round. I can tell this is going to be fun."

11

"It's not fun. It's work," she snapped back at him.

"Okay." He was still chuckling. "Tote that barge and lift that bale, Lily. Let's go to work."

Trent led her over to the car, which had been hidden behind a billowing sheet of snow. He held the door open for Lily and she slid in, relieved to be out of the biting snow at last and hoping, now that they were finally on their way, that he would be more reasonable. She threw her case in the back seat.

Trent slipped behind the wheel and turned the ignition key. The car caught immediately, and he headed out to the road—or what was probably the road. The snow had obscured its boundaries. Trent pushed the button that started the wipers and they swished back and forth across the windshield, pushing aside mounds of flakes that were immediately replaced by more mounds of flakes. Lily peered through the windshield and tried to make out the shapes of houses, or even trees, by the roadside, but all she could see was an expanse of white. It was as if a curtain of white velvet had been drawn all around them. There was nothing but white and white and more white.

"This is one hell of a storm," Trent said as he inched the car along, his long lanky body crouched over the steering wheel.

"I'm going to turn the radio on. Let's see what the weatherman has to say." Lily reached over, but Trent grabbed her hand before she could push the button.

"Lily, I don't need a weatherman to tell me what the weather is. We're in a blizzard—a real nor'easter—and nothing the weatherman says is going to help our situation." He said it very matter-of-factly.

"But he can tell us when it's going to stop, or something," she finished lamely. Trent's hand was still clutching hers. His warm fingers had been massaging her cold ones while he spoke, and the electricity passing between them felt strong enough to give her brain damage. She tried to pull her hand away, but he held tight.

"I'll tell you when it's going to stop. After about two feet of snow's been dropped out of the sky. And then we'll have bright blue skies and temperatures in the teens. There's your weather forecast. Feel better?" He let her hand go.

Lily eyed him uneasily. "How do you know all that?" she asked. She had assumed he was a New York City model whose knowledge of the weather was limited to knowing that when it rained you took a cab and when it didn't you walked. He was beginning to blast to bits her theory that he was just a mindless hunk of meat with not too much between the ears.

"I grew up in Connecticut, not far from here. We used to get these kinds of storms when I was a kid."

"Oh." Lily was struck silent. Maybe she was underestimating Trent. Maybe he did have something between the ears after all. The situation as she had originally perceived it was beginning to change. But still, she was the famous writer and he wasn't. He couldn't top her there.

"How far is it to Litchfield?" Lily asked to change the subject.

"About thirty miles, and at the rate we're going it'll take well over an hour to get there. Why don't you just sit back and let me do the driving? I'll get us there, and there's no reason to worry your—"

"My pretty little head?" Lily broke in to complete his sentence.

Trent looked at her sharply. "I wasn't going to say that."

As Lily looked at him, she realized that he was right. He hadn't been going to say that; she had just been looking for an excuse to get his goat because his mere existence irritated her, and now she couldn't back down.

"You certainly were. But I'm used to that." Lily was so uncomfortable that she just started rattling along. "Men are always saying those kinds of things to me. Just because my books are what critics like to call 'light reading,' men assume I don't have a brain in my head.

But my books are hard to do. You have to have the right kind of style and tone. The plots are very complicated, and I spend—"

"Okay, Lily, I get the picture," Trent interrupted. "You're not Dostoevski and neither am I."

Lily wondered what he meant by that. "You're not a writer, are you? I thought you were a model." She hoped against hope that her suspicion was wrong. She didn't want to be trapped in a car with Trent Daily while he told her, point by point, what was wrong with her books, because she was sure that that was exactly what he had planned for her.

"I am a writer," Trent said intensely, "but I write about serious subjects, and unfortunately, that means I don't make much money. In fact, I don't make any money writing because I've never been published."

"Oh," Lily said. She hoped he wasn't going to tell her what his books were like. They were probably very depressing, and it was depressing enough to be stuck in the car with him.

"I've never read any of your books," he went on, "but I guess I can figure out what they're like. They're bathtub books. If they fall in the tub and get wet, it's okay, because they're not worth saving." Touché, he was probably saying to himself.

"Take that back!" Lily was so angry that she reached over and yanked on Trent's earlobe, just like she used to do to her older brother Alex when he teased her, since it was the only way she could ever get him to stop. Trent twisted and looked at her, his eyes wide and surprised. He hadn't expected that. With his eyes on Lily instead of the road, he accidentally let the car slide out of control and plow into a snowbank. He slammed on the brakes.

"Would you like to walk the rest of the way, Lily? I doubt you'll get far in those heels." He rubbed his earlobe gingerly.

Lily's spirits sank. He was right. She was stuck with Trent Daily because she *couldn't* walk. She'd freeze to death or be buried alive in the snow before she went even half a mile.

"No, I'm not going to walk." Lily sat straight in her seat and folded her hands in her lap to calm her nerves. "But I would like to know one thing, Trent. Why did you take this job playing my husband if you have so little respect for my writing? I should think it would be demeaning."

"I need the money," Trent said shortly, his eyes evading hers.

"Oh . . . well . . ." Lily was taken aback. She didn't know what to say. There had never been even one second in her life when she had needed money; it had always been there. She felt a small stab of sympathy for Trent. It was hard being a writer, even when you knew that what you wrote was going to be published. It could be a lonely, solitary life. But to write and know that no one besides a few friends would ever see it, that must be difficult to accept. But still, Trent shouldn't be so antagonistic toward the kind of books she wrote. If she could have written serious books she would have, but she wrote mystery novels because she had a flair for them. And he should be able to understand that.

"Well, what do you do for a living?" she asked him, genuinely curious. She wondered how an unpublished writer supported himself.

"I have a friend in the moving business. I move people's furniture."

That explained his well-muscled legs and broad chest. Crouching over a typewriter wasn't exactly body-building exercise.

"Hm, a mover and a writer. What an interesting combination," she observed sarcastically.

"You don't need the money, do you, Lily?" Trent asked, his eyes focusing on her sable coat. "Why are you doing this?"

Lily almost wanted to say that she had been bamboozled into it, because Trent was right, she didn't need the money. When her agent, Bev Simmons, had called her and told her about Fountaine's fantastically lucrative offer, and then said that since her books were about a mystery-solving couple, Fountaine *assumed* she was married and that the whole endorsement *depended* on her being married, she had been just as eager as Bev to hire a husband and fake it. It had actually looked like fun.

Fountaine's advertising concept demanded a couple, since the campaign was aimed at the upwardly mobile young marrieds who were just beginning to drink wine. And as Bev had said, "Who wants to watch a single lady sitting around getting loaded all by herself?" And then Bev had dared her. "You're not going to let the mere fact that you don't actually have a husband stand in your way, are you, Lily?"

Never, to her chagrin, having been one to refuse a dare, Lily had practically ordered Bev to find her a suitable "husband," pronto. Trent was a friend of someone who worked with Bev, and Bev had hired him at first sight. She'd told Lily that he'd be perfect. How could Bev have been so wrong? Lily was really beginning to regret her impulsiveness about getting involved with what had seemed, a few weeks ago, such a fantastic idea. She and Bev had even joked about it. They'd called it her "Madison Avenue marriage." Now she cringed at the thought of it. Casting a surreptitious glance at Trent, she reminded herself that theirs was a "marriage" made strictly for business. If she could conduct herself accordingly, so could he. But then she looked at him again, and at the sight of his long black lashes and the purple eyes they shaded, she began to have doubts.

Lawrence Lansden—the name they'd cooked up for him—was a figment of her imagination, a beautiful and lucrative dream, but Trent Daily . . . Well, he was beginning to seem more like a nightmare.

Lily decided to be as truthful as possible with Trent. Perhaps if she leveled with him, he'd stop being so annoying.

"I'm doing it for my publisher and my agent, mostly. When I make money, my agent makes money too, and if people see me on television, even if it's just drinking wine, they'll think of my books and, I hope, buy one the next time they're in a bookstore."

"Ah, selling out to the masses . . ." Trent let his inflammatory statement dangle.

"What!" Lily exclaimed. There was no use in being truthful with Trent Daily. He was determined to be a royal pain in the neck.

"That's okay, Lily. I'm sure my mom's not the only one who reads your books in the bathtub." His voice changed to mimic a TV announcer's. "Now, for all you bathtub readers out there—Lily Lansden and today's husband, Lawrence." His voice changed back. "Hey, maybe they should film us drinking champagne in a bubble bath; that would tie it all in so nicely." He was really enjoying himself, Lily could see, making jokes at her expense.

"Look, Trent. I don't care if your mother reads my books in the shower! I do not sell out. I write what I write because it amuses me and a lot of other people too." He was looking at her with the most flagrantly false attempt at looking sincere that she had ever seen, and she lost her temper again. "Who are you to say that I sell out? You've never even been published. You don't know anything." Lily was rising out of her seat and pushing herself up close to Trent, pointing agitatedly at his face with her index finger. "You're a big know-nothing," she finished childishly, suddenly left at a loss for words by his closeness.

Trent grabbed her finger quickly before she had a chance to lower her hand, and pressed it heatedly against his lips. "Oh, Lily love, you're so lovely when you're angry. May I kiss this finger? This finger that, along with the four others, pens those monuments to modern literature, those landmarks of literary language, those definitive delights . . ." He leered at her with fake lasciviousness, sarcasm dripping like cyanide-laced honey from his sardonic words.

"Oh, you . . ." Lily grabbed her finger away from Trent's lips. "Start this car. Right now. The sooner we get to the house, the sooner I'll be able to get away from you."

"Well, I wish you'd make up your mind." Trent wrenched the steering wheel sharply to the left and pressed down on the accelerator, but the car stayed where it was, the wheels spinning helplessly on the slick snow.

"We're stuck!" Lily covered her face with her hands and slid down into her seat. She couldn't believe it! She was stuck in the middle of nowhere, in more snow than she had ever seen in her entire life, with the most insufferable man she had ever met. Why had she said yes to her agent? This was turning into a full-fledged disaster!

"I'll take care of this." Trent jumped out of the car and ran to the rear to check the tires, while Lily cursed herself for momentarily losing her head. From now on, she vowed, she would keep her cool. No matter what happened, she wasn't going to let Trent Daily have the satisfaction of seeing her fall to pieces.

Trent pulled open his door and entered the car in a whoosh of snowflakes and frigid air. Lily presented her newly calmed demeanor.

"How does it look?" she asked, as if she couldn't care less, as if getting stuck in snowstorms was something she did all the time.

"Well, Lily," Trent replied, shaking snow from the shock of black hair that brushed his right eye and wiping melted flakes from his cheeks, "you're the one who's always getting her characters out of scrapes. How do you suggest we get out of this one?"

Lily was struck again by the force of his intensely masculine presence, but she remained calm. "What's the problem?"

"We're stuck," Trent answered as if she didn't know.

"I know we're stuck." She was trying to think. She had never even driven a car. Who needed a car in New York? You took taxis—and she flew or was driven everywhere else. She took a lame stab. "Maybe we could call a garage?"

"What? With my shoe phone?" Trent was trying not to laugh, she could tell.

"Well . . ." What did you do when you were stuck in snow? "Well . . ." Suddenly it came to her. "You push, and I'll drive us out of it."

"A masterful idea, Lily. I'm surprised I didn't think of it myself." He was so sarcastic, yet his body was so lithe and graceful, and his eyes so like onyx and sparkling amethyst, and his mouth so warm and . . . Lily's thoughts had rambled into dangerous territory. Fortunately, Trent hadn't noticed.

"All right, then. Just steer to the left and push down on the gas when I tell you to." He started to lean against his door, as if he were about to exit. "Scoot over this way and you won't have to go outside."

Thinking that he was on his way out, Lily slid over to his side. But Trent stayed in place, and their hips bumped against each other, though too quickly and sharply to be provocative.

"My, my, Lily, you *are* eager. Can't you wait till we get to the house?" Trent's expression was deadpan.

"No, I can't," she replied, her face just as emotionless as his, although her body was heating up again at such close contact. "Because as soon as I get there, I'm going to run to the room furthest away from yours and only come out when the director says 'Action.'"

"Lily . . ." Trent heaved a sardonic sigh. "I don't know why I ever married you. You're a hard, hard woman," he said as he got out of the car.

Lily slid over behind the wheel and cracked the side window an inch or two so she could hear Trent's directions, then sighed. Being so close to him was disconcerting; her shaky knees were all the proof she needed of his physical effect upon her. But why did he have to be so unpleasant, so antagonistic? If only his personality matched his looks she wouldn't mind playing at being his wife; it might even be fun. But now the next few days with him stretched before her like an ordeal that would involve hours of teeth-gritting. It would be worth it, though. The exposure she and her books would get from being on television would be worth millions of dollars in free publicity. Nerve-wracking or not, filming this commercial with Trent Daily was going to be worth whatever amount of discomfort it involved.

"Okay, Lily!" Trent yelled. "Give it some gas."

She pressed down on the accelerator, and as the engine gunned, Trent pushed against the car. It bounced and the wheels spun and caught for a second. The car lurched forward a few inches; then the wheels spun again.

"Good, you're doing fine," Trent encouraged. "Again."

She repeated the procedure with the same result.

"Again!" Trent yelled.

She accelerated again, but this time the wheels just spun.

"Okay. Stop." Trent came over to the window. "Your idea bombed."

"Do you have a better one?"

"We're not getting enough traction. We need something under the wheels. Let's make a deal." Trent's face assumed a devilish mien, and Lily winced, wondering what the deal was going to be.

"I can give up my shirt for the left tire. What can you give for the right?"

Lily suspected a plan on Trent's part to get her out of her clothes.

"Is this really necessary?" she challenged him.

"I'm afraid it is, Lily love." He pressed his face close to the window. "Don't you have anything to offer?"

She really had nothing to offer besides the clothes on

her back, and she wasn't about to volunteer her teal blue silk dress. But wait . . . She had a suitcase full of clothes. Perhaps she could spare something . . . for a price.

"I have something," she stated boldly. "But only on one condition."

"What's that?" Trent looked interested.

"That you stop calling me 'Lily love.' I don't like it." It seemed that there was only one way to keep a man like Trent Daily in line: wheeling and dealing for decent behavior.

"It's a deal, Lily," Trent agreed. "But you know I can come up with other nicknames for you. Like Lily snookums, and Lily sweetie, and Lily long legs . . ."

"You do and I'll find another husband, Trent Daily! You're expendable, you know. I'm the famous writer, not you."

"As I'm sure you'll be constantly reminding me," Trent said in resignation. "All right, Lily, no more nicknames. Now, may I have the clothing you promised? I'll turn my head."

"You don't have to, smarty; it's in my case." Lily turned, opened her suitcase and pulled out the first thing she touched. It was her nightgown—a pale peach satin and lace affair. It was more expendable than her jeans, so she decided to sacrifice it. She threw it out the window, and Trent caught it, then held it up and examined it closely.

"What lovely taste you have, Lily. Even in your underwear. I had no idea you'd be giving me something this . . . intimate. I don't know if I can bear to put it underneath the wheel where it will be sullied and torn and . . ."

Lily came to a boil. "Just take it and do what you have to do. Anything, just so we can get out of here and I can get away from you."

"I appreciate the sacrifice you're making, Lily, as I'm sure you'll appreciate mine."

In the middle of thousands of whirling snowflakes, and

with the air a temperature that would have had the abominable snowman's teeth chattering, Trent pulled off his down jacket, unbuttoned his shirt, and ripped it away to expose his lithe, powerful chest.

Not one for false modesty, Lily observed to herself as she watched the muscles rippling across the smooth, strong expanse of his chest. With his black hair, wide cheekbones and proud carriage, Trent could almost have been mistaken for an Indian brave if his skin hadn't been so light. As he stood there in the storm, his ivory flesh exposed to the strong wind and its burden of stinging snow, he was profoundly male, his pale skin almost the color of fine, hard marble. What a strange, strange man, Lily thought. To be so beautiful and so . . . so unbearable, she finished as reality impinged.

Noticing her appraisal of his body, Trent gave her an amused wink, slipped his jacket back on and ran to the rear of the car.

How mortifying! Lily cringed and prayed that he'd be so involved with the car that he'd forget about her interest in him when he got back inside.

After a minute or so he yelled at her to give the car some gas. The wheels caught immediately and Lily steered back onto the road. They were finally on their way.

"Don't stop," Trent yelled. "I'll jump in and you scoot over again."

Lily did as she was told. She was so happy to be moving again that she had no reason to protest. Trent jumped in, she scooted over, and they headed down the road.

"Sorry about your gown. I'll buy you a new one later."

"That's not necessary. It's not your fault," Lily said graciously.

"Oh, I'm glad you see it that way. At last we agree on something—that it was your fault we got stuck."

"My fault!" Lily forgot her vow to remain calm and her voice rose excitedly. "How do you figure that?"

"Well, you were the one who made me run off the road, weren't you? If you had just let me drive, it never would have happened."

"If you're so clever, Trent," Lily asked, "why didn't you just keep your eyes on the road and ignore me?"

"What! And risk the further wrath of Lily Lansden? And besides, that's not the point," he said.

"What is the point?"

"That I got us out of the mess you got us into. You owe me one, Lily, and I intend to collect." His look was infinitely suggestive.

"It'll be snowing in July before you ever collect anything from me, Trent Daily," she replied.

"Is that so?" he asked curiously.

"Yes," Lily replied with finality.

It was obvious that they were at a standoff. Minutes passed, and neither Lily nor Trent said a word. The silence began to get on Lily's nerves. It was even worse than the bickering. Maybe if they could call a truce for the time being this whole experience could at least be bearable. Perhaps Lily should be big about it and make the first move toward peace; it might give her the upper hand if she were the reasonable one. She could hardly believe how scheming she had become, but she knew she could never let her guard down with a man like Trent, not even for a second.

"Trent," Lily began sweetly, "can we call it quits? I can't stand all this arguing. Besides, if we're going to be working together, we have to get along—at least superficially. If we keep up like this, Fountaine's going to know we're fakers, and then we'll both be sunk." Lily was so proud of herself for being the voice of reason. It was an attitude she rarely displayed; usually she was wild and giddy and everyone else had to be calm around her. She was so proud that she hardly cared what Trent had to say in reply.

"I agree with you about trying to get along, Lily." Trent gazed at her with a look that almost spoke of a glimmer of respect beneath its surface. "But I don't agree that if we're constantly bickering, Fountaine will think we're fakers. Do you really want to play at being lovey-dovey all the time? That's a sure giveaway."

"But married people are supposed to be lovey-dovey. That's why they're married. They love each other." Trent was starting to confuse her again.

"What planet have you been living on, Lily? Married people fight like blazes. *That's* why they're married. They know how to fight with each other better than with anyone else."

Lily couldn't decide if he meant what he said or was just being sarcastic. "If you mean it, that's an awful thing to say," Lily replied.

"Well, it's true. My parents fought all the time. And they had a very happy marriage."

"They were happy?" Somehow Lily knew that beneath the cynicism Trent was getting at something important.

"Yes. They were happy. They were both very creative, very vital people, and their personalities were very strong. Naturally they clashed. Only the truly dull don't fight. They're not interested in anything, so how could they?"

Lily remained quiet. She had no smart answer to what Trent had just said. It made her think about James Preston, her old boyfriend. Or was he still her boyfriend? He'd left town several months ago, and now they seemed to have drifted apart. At least, James had drifted. In her heart, Lily still expected him to return. Someday.

She and James had never fought, and they could never have been accused of being dull. They had agreed on everything. They both had the same favorite restaurants and the same favorite people; they even drank the same drink—a very dry, very cold martini with a twist. They had never even been sharp with each other. Maybe Trent liked to think that people in love fought because he liked to fight, although it didn't seem to make any difference whether he was in love or not. Probably he was bad tempered with everyone.

Lily couldn't stand it. "But James and I never fought," she stated, and then regretted her impulsiveness.

Trent looked at her sharply. "James? Don't tell me there really is a Mr. Lansden?"

"No, Trent, the title's yours, at least for the next few days," Lily answered smartly. "James was a b—— a friend of mine, and we never fought." Now she felt really dumb. The whole purpose of bringing up James had been to prove that she had been in love with someone and they hadn't fought. But for some strange reason her mouth just wouldn't let her say "boyfriend" when it came to describing James, as if she felt she had to keep him a secret from Trent. Or maybe it was because thinking of James made her feel so awful.

She had used James as the model for Dash Chadbourne and had always fancied herself as Dana, his wife, when she wrote her books about the glamorous, mystery-solving couple. She and James had gone everywhere and done everything together; they'd even planned to be married, except for some reason their plans were always postponed—by James. Lily had thought they were the perfect couple until suddenly he had decided to move to Los Angeles, of all places, and take a job with a newspaper. His letters and phone calls had been sporadic from the first, and then, a month or so ago, had finally stopped. Lily knew that, in the popular lingo, she had been "dumped." What could be more humiliating?

Trent pressed on. "Lily, I didn't say friends fought. I said lovers fought. So which was he, a friend or a lover?" Trent's eyes were almost indigo, his gaze was so intense.

Why couldn't she just say that he had been her lover and be done with it? But something in the intensity of Trent's gaze increased her reluctance to talk about James even more. She couldn't get her tongue to touch the roof of her mouth to begin the *l* for lover. Instead she forced air between her lips and said, "Friend."

"Well then . . ." Trent let the matter drop, as if he knew he had touched a truly sensitive spot, and not just one that was vulnerable to a naughty taunt or some mild teasing.

Lily was silent for a long time, and Trent seemed to respect her quiet mood, because he too kept his tongue.

Finally he said softly, "You're awfully quiet."

"Oh. I was just thinking about all this snow. When does it stop? And when will we be there?"

"We're almost there now. In fact, this road here" —Trent made a sharp left—"is the one that takes us to Litchfield."

Lily was relieved to have something new to think about, and she perked up immediately. She had only heard a little bit about the house from Bev, but what she had heard sounded wonderful. Even though Albert Fountaine's winery was in upstate New York, he had chosen the house in Connecticut, which belonged to some friends of his, because it would be so photogenic. It was perched on a hill overlooking the largest lake in the state, and it was, Bev had said, the kind of country house that people made movies about. Lily's curiosity about what it would really look like made her more and more eager to get there, and she began to lean forward in her seat like an excited child.

Trent glanced over at her and laughed. "Lily, sit back. You're like a kid going to summer camp for the first time. Leaning forward is not going to get you there any faster. But tell me, are you more excited about seeing the house or about getting rid of me?"

Trent looked at her as he spoke, and this time she felt as if he sincerely wanted to know and would be disappointed if the answer was that she wanted to get away from him. But she couldn't let her guard down and tell him how she really felt, that in a strange, as yet indefinable way, he interested her, and that his mere presence was exciting. She avoided the true answer by giving an evasive one. "Both," she said ingenuously, and laughed.

Trent looked at her, seemed to understand, and laughed along with her.

They had made their truce.

2

∽◦◦◦◦◦◦◦◦◦◦◦∾

Finally, after several turns that took them onto narrower and curvier country roads, the house came into view at the crest of a hill. It was a boxy, clapboard, two-story building with low wings extending on either side of its four-columned front. It was painted a creamy white, and Lily could see the windows with their shiny black shutters peeking out from between a line of snow-flecked firs. Two chimneys, one on either end of the main building's roof, anchored the house onto its snowy patch of land and gave it an air of having been there for centuries. It had that stable, solid, been-through-it-all-and-come-out-intact kind of feel about it. To that house, Lily mused, today's snowstorm was nothing out of the ordinary, and she felt more secure knowing that this was where she'd be staying for the next few days. She'd feel a lot *more* secure, however, if she thought that Bev, Albert Fountaine and the camera crew were going to make it up to the house that night as they'd planned. Now that it was getting dark and the snow was still falling as if it would never stop, Lily was beginning to doubt that they would. What if she were stranded with Trent for the evening? At the rate Trent was going, who knew what could happen?

Trent pulled into the circular driveway and stopped beneath a snow-blanketed maple tree.

"Here we are, Lily." He turned off the ignition and looked at her meaningfully. "I wouldn't want you getting your dainty little feet cold and wet again, so what do you say we do the traditional thing?"

Lily looked at him warily. What was he talking about?

"Don't move. I'll come over to your side and open your door."

Lily knew he was going to try to pull some kind of smart stunt, but what was it?

Trent came over to her door, opened it, and before she even had a millisecond to protest, he had scooped her out of the seat and into his arms.

"Trent, what is this? What do you think you're doing?" She struggled against him, but she couldn't escape the arms that held her so tightly. She could feel his heart pounding beneath his jacket, its throbbing rhythm an exact match to her own.

"I'm carrying the bride over the threshold. Isn't that how it's supposed to go?" His eyes blazed into her own, and a wry smile lifted the corners of his full mouth.

Lily pressed her hands against his chest and then began to elbow him, trying to find a weak spot. "Trent, you're going too far. This is absolutely ridiculous. Please put me down."

"Are you sure?" he teased wickedly. "If I do, you'll be standing in about twelve inches of very cold and very wet snow, and your feet just won't approve, not to mention how those lovely legs of yours will feel."

Lily's elbow finally made contact with a tender spot right beneath Trent's armpit. "Ouch!" he yelled. It was the first sincere emotion she'd gotten out of him yet. "That hurt!" He immediately released her squirming body.

Lily flailed her arms and legs in midair, hoping she'd have the grace of a cat and land on her feet. She did, but not before she sank into at least a foot of snow, just as Trent had promised.

"Ow! That's cold!" She had to grab onto Trent to keep her balance.

"Back for more?" he asked. "And so soon?"

He pressed himself closely against her, his entire length molding itself against her body as he drew her mouth up to his. His lips touched hers softly, and he nibbled and licked at her mouth, willing it into a kiss that promised such depth and passion that Lily involuntarily pulled him even closer. Their lips moved together in a deeply sensuous rhythm as Trent's hands wandered to her back and, through the thick sable fur, massaged her into compliance. They kissed heatedly for what could have been hours, it was so deliciously slow and pleasurable, the kiss intensifying as Trent parted her lips with his tongue and explored the ripe interior of her mouth. It was like nothing Lily had ever experienced before. They seemed to be rising to the heavens together in a moment of rapturous delight, absolutely heedless of the snow falling on them softly, insistently, hitting their heads and faces with downy flakes that melted instantaneously in the heat generated by their embrace.

Trent moved against Lily even more insistently, his long muscled legs pressing against her soft thighs. But just when the pleasure had heightened to almost unbearable proportions, something in Lily's mind snapped her back to reality. She remembered Trent's condescending insinuations about her books, and his merciless teasing. She pulled away from him abruptly.

"What do you think you're doing?" she shouted angrily, wanting to rub her lips with the back of her hand to wipe the heat and the memory of his kiss away in one quick swipe.

"I'm sealing our pact," he said calmly.

"What pact?"

"The one we made back in the car that we'd act like husband and wife. Our truce."

She overcame her flustered nerves with a quick rush of self-control. "That truce we made, Trent, was merely for show—for everyone else, not for us—and since no one else is here, it doesn't apply."

Trent stared at her unbelievingly, and then his expression turned crafty. "All right, Lily, if you want to deny your feelings toward me. . . ."

"What feelings?" Lily demanded.

"You protest too much, Lily. I think you like me to kiss you. I can see sparks in your eyes when I do."

"Sparks! Are you crazy? What you're seeing in my eyes is pure, unadulterated annoyance at your conceited, boorish personality. I'd say that I loathe you, but that would be trite, and I know how you must feel about triteness. It's probably a sin against 'great literature,' which you, judging from your attitude toward my work, seem to be upholding single-handedly. I think you're an arrogant, haughty, insolent—"

"Lily, you're sounding like a thesaurus. I get the message."

Lily had finally had enough of Trent's particular brand of one-upmanship. She turned and tried to run toward the front door, but the snow was so deep that all she could manage was a comically awkward trudge. It was so like her to fly off the handle and then bolt. It reminded her of her childhood days, when she would run away from the things that bothered or frightened her, but she couldn't help herself. Trent's kiss had struck a chord deep within and stirred longings so profound and previously repressed that she was actually scared.

She turned the brass doorknob and quickly stepped inside, then leaned against the door's comforting solidity to catch her breath. In front of her was a scene so charming and picturesque that she half expected Bing Crosby to come sauntering around a corner and welcome her to Holiday Inn. A central staircase curved graciously upward in front of her. To the right was a huge stone fireplace stacked with wood awaiting only a match's touch to turn it into a blazing, crackling fire. Beneath her feet were wide polished boards and an enormous oriental rug filled with flowers and birds and sinuous arabesques in jewel-like colors. Lounging invitingly before the fire was a long couch upholstered in striped satin, and a pair of easy chairs with curving lyre-shaped backs and graceful thin legs whose arched eagle claws grasped highly polished balls of finely grained cherry. The living room stretched from one side of the house to the other, and the whole opposite wall was a floor-to-ceiling window that framed a breathtaking view of the countryside.

Outside, by the light of a full, beaming moon, the snow still fell, covering the fir trees until their branches dipped close to the ground under the heavy weight of their snowy burden. Shining in the moon's glow were undulating hills as far as the eye could see, and nestled in their center was a lake that shimmered in the moonlight. Its luminous beauty calmed her nerves. She forgot that she was running away from Trent and just sat in front of the window, lost in contemplation of such pure, natural beauty.

A sharp ringing brought Lily back to reality. It was the telephone, and she knew she had better answer it in case it was her agent, or Fountaine, or the crew. She ran into the vestibule and picked up the receiver.

"Hello."

"Lily. My God, you're there!"

It was Bev, the person who had gotten her into this ridiculous situation. "Of course I'm here. I'm supposed to be here. Where are you?"

"I'm in New York."

"New York! Bev, you're supposed to be here too!"

"I know I am, but the trains have stopped running," Bev said simply.

"You're not coming?" Lily asked.

"Not unless I can buy a pair of snowshoes. No, of course I'm not. How can I?"

"Oh, Bev." Lily collapsed into the nearest chair. "I'm here all alone." She almost began to cry, but her pride held back the tears.

"What happened to what's his name . . . Lawrence? Didn't he pick you up?"

"Yes, he did. That's the problem. Oh, Bev, how could

you have picked him to be my husband? I hate him," Lily
wailed.

"But I thought he was nice, and very handsome."

"He's not handsome, he's a beast. He's rude and
snide and . . . oh, Bev, he's awful."

"Lily . . ." Bev's voice took on the tone of a mother
scolding a child. "You're just upset about all the snow.
Maybe you're hungry."

"I'm not hungry, I'm harassed. When will the crew be
here?"

"That's just it, Lil," Bev said calmly. Giving bad news
always brought out the calmness in people, Lily thought.
They thought that if they stayed calm, the person they
were breaking the bad news to would stay calm along
with them.

"The crew's here in New York too. They headed out,
but had to turn back. The roads are closed."

"You mean I'm stuck here with him? Oh, Bev, why
couldn't you have picked someone to be my husband
who was pretty but dumb? This man thinks he knows
everything. He thinks he's some kind of great, unknown
literary artist. He criticizes my books; he makes fun of the
way I dress. He's a nightmare."

"Lily, you're not sounding like yourself at all. You're
sounding like some kind of hysterical shrew. Now, come
on. Where's that old Lansden spunk? You've got to grit
your teeth and tough it out. It's too late to get a new
husband." Bev's tone was firm, and something in its
depths told Lily that she had better calm down and do
just as Bev said. Bev was too good an agent to have to
put up with a difficult client, even if the client was such a
well-known and moneymaking one as Lily. And Bev was
right. She wasn't acting like herself at all. Trent *had*
turned her into a hysterical shrew with his taunting and
teasing. She'd have to get control of herself and find
some way of fighting back.

"You're not going anywhere," Bev went on, "so you'll
just have to make the best of things."

"I figured that one out a while ago. I just didn't think I'd have to spend the night alone with *him.*"

"Just make excuses and go to bed early," Bev said like the reasonable woman she was. *"If* he's that vile."

Lily had to tell Bev what the real problem was. "That would be fine, but he likes to play at being my husband. He seems to think we should *really* act like we're married."

Bev understood immediately. "You're kidding!"

"Unh-unh," Lily replied, relieved at finally having someone besides Trent to talk to, someone who would understand her predicament instead of teasing her about it. "I've been fighting him off ever since I met him this afternoon. He's obsessed with the idea."

"Well, use that Lansden charm, Lily. Or, even better, be flaky and flighty. If he's such an egghead, that's sure to turn him off."

"Now, there's an idea!" For some silly reason she had been resenting Trent's thinking she was less than an intellectual giant. What if she used his disdain of her to her own purposes? She could act so flighty, so dumb and dull witted, that he'd *want* to stay away from her. Lily was immediately cheered. "Like giving vinegar to flies," she joked, remembering the old saying about catching more flies with honey.

"Great. That's just the thing. Now I hear the old Lily talking."

"When will I see you?" Lily asked.

"I'll try to make it tomorrow, but if the roads are out . . ."

"Oh, Bev . . ." Panic crept back into Lily's voice. "I can't stand another day like this!"

"Remember what we said now: vinegar."

Just as Bev finished her sentence, the front door opened and Trent entered.

"Yes, I know. Well, Bev," Lily said brightly, so Trent wouldn't see her fear, "see you soon."

"Thatta girl," Bev responded. "Go to it!"

Trent approached. "Who was that?" he asked when Lily hung up the phone.

"Oh, that was my agent." Lily took a deep breath and decided to plunge right into the flaky act. "She says she's not coming. Unless she can buy some snowshoes. But I don't think she can find any. Well, maybe she could, but I don't think she really meant it. I guess she's not coming." Lily smiled up at Trent in that bright, cheery kind of way that only the truly air-headed can manage.

Trent looked at her askance. "I would have thought you'd be angry about that. It looks like we're going to be here alone."

"Oh, what difference does it make?" Lily was smiling so hard that she thought her cheeks would split. She didn't know how far she could push this flaky business, but she'd press on until she got a sign from Trent that she'd gone too far. "You're here, and you know about those woodsy kinds of things, so I feel perfectly safe."

Trent looked at her as if something was drastically wrong. This wasn't the feisty Lily he had gotten accustomed to. "Did your agent say anything about the rest of the crew? Or the sponsor?"

"They're not coming either. It's just you and me." She looked up at him from beneath her lashes and would have batted them, but that was one trick that, unfortunately, she'd never learned.

"Would you get my bag from the car? My poor little feet are just too tired to make it all on their little own."

She had never seen a lip curl in disgust before; in fact, she had always thought that was something writers made up, but she could have sworn that Trent's lip lifted ever so slightly at one corner.

"All right." He eyed her as if she were some kind of strange new creature. "But sit down right away. Your poor little body obviously can't stand the strain much longer, and I'd hate to see you swoon." Trent left quickly, as if he couldn't wait to remove himself from her presence.

Lily walked lightly toward the window. Bev was a genius! The one thing a man with Trent Daily's kind of intellectual pretentions couldn't stand was a woman who seemed completely frivolous and banal. As soon as she was sure he was out of earshot, Lily let out a peal of laughter. She wouldn't have to worry about Trent anymore. He couldn't even stand to be in the same room with her!

Minutes passed, and Trent didn't return. Lily sat in an armchair, contemplating the scene outside the windows. She felt as if she were a child experiencing snow for the first time. Of course, since she had grown up in New York City, she *had* seen snow before, but snow falling between skyscrapers and settling on the sidewalks and streets and turning into nasty slippery slush was quite different from snow in the country. Here it seemed to settle softly into swollen curves that blanketed everything —trees, hills, ponds, the house itself—as if it were sealing things away from the rest of the world.

Lily sighed. If only she were sealed in, isolated with someone she could care about, whose company she could enjoy, instead of with Trent Daily. But, she had to admit, there had been a moment, while they were in the car, when she had seen something in him that she had liked, something that was thoughtful and serious and perceptive. Why did he try to hide that part of himself by being rude and condescending—when he wasn't being a malicious tease? And his snobbery about her "kind of books" was so unnecessary. If he felt as strongly as he seemed to about literature, and if he truly felt that his writing was important, why did he think that attacking Lily would somehow help his cause? His words would speak for themselves . . . if they were ever published. Lily had found a grain of truth. That was why he was rude: he resented her because she was published and he wasn't, because he had something important to say— supposedly—and she didn't.

Lily sighed once more. James had encouraged her writing. He had helped her think up plots and characters, and when she had to do research that involved traveling, he had gone along with her eagerly, always interested in what new places were waiting to be discovered. He had been the perfect companion. Lily's thoughts stopped short. Every time she thought about James she thought the same thing—that they had been perfect together. But then came the same nagging conclusion—that even so, he had left her. If they had been so perfect together, why had he taken that newspaper job out in Los Angeles when it meant leaving her; and why had it been understood, without one word between them, that she shouldn't relocate to be with him? If they had been so happy together, why had he wanted to go away? And why had the phone calls and letters stopped after he had been gone for only a few months? It just didn't make sense. Unless . . . Lily's stomach did a flip-flop as she forced herself to face the truth. He must have found someone else. They hadn't been as perfect together as she had thought.

So here she was, stuck with Trent Daily, having to act like a dingbat so he'd stop trying to kiss her. Suddenly Lily saw the ludicrousness of the situation. Why shouldn't she want Trent to kiss her? He was certainly attractive, and she had to admit that none of James's numerous kisses had ever made her feel as shivery and excited as just one of Trent's had. But they couldn't even talk about the weather without getting into an argument. He was such a difficult man. But did that mean that she had to be difficult too? Maybe he just couldn't help it, and here she was being a dingbat on purpose. Already she was getting tired of the silly game she was playing with Trent. It was so demeaning to play dumb, especially when you knew you were far from it. There had to be a better way to handle him.

Lily settled further into the chair and pulled her fur

closer to her body. It was getting chillier and chillier in the house. When would Trent return to start the fire? Perhaps she should start it herself. Wouldn't he be surprised to know that she could do something as practical as lighting a fire?

On the hearth she found a box of matches. Although Lily had no experience lighting fires, she reasoned that all it required was lighting the match and touching it to the kindling stacked neatly beneath the larger logs. She lit the match, touched the kindling and was relieved when the flame took. She pulled a chair up to the fireplace and stretched her feet out toward the flickering flames. Warmth at last!

But something was wrong. The smoke, which should have been coiling up into the chimney, was instead rolling in choking billows into the room. She jumped up and began to wave her arms like a crazed chicken flapping its wings, coughing as her eyes smarted and teared from the bitter bite of the smoke.

She heard the front door opening.

"What the . . . ?" Trent rushed over to the fireplace, grabbed a poker and, forcing it up the chimney shaft, yanked at something that gave a grating, metallic groan. Smoke roiled up into the chimney and the room began to clear.

Lily stood next to him, not daring to look at his face. She had thought she had to pretend to be dumb, when actually, she really had been all along. Now she had shown even herself that she was a dim-witted ninny who didn't even know how to light a fire.

"What were you trying to do, Lily? Burn us down?" Trent asked calmly, as if he half expected that she did this kind of thing all the time.

"No." Lily's first response was to rear up and defend herself; then she realized that she had to play along with her mistake. "I was cold, so I decided to start a fire," she said with the simplicity of an idiot.

"Don't you know about flues? They have to be

opened so the smoke can get out. If I hadn't come along when I did . . ."

"I know, Trent." Lily didn't have to feign her embarrassment. "I'm sorry. I just thought you lit the match and that was that." She felt like such a fool.

"Just leave the fire starting to me from now on. I'm going to find us some dinner." He left for the kitchen, then returned in a few minutes with some wonderful-looking ham on thick slabs of home-baked bread.

"Good thing the cupboard wasn't bare. Someone around here is a terrific cook," he said nonchalantly as he handed her a sandwich. "I don't suppose you cook?"

"No," Lily said honestly. The disaster with the fire had humbled her. "I don't pretend to be a cook. I'm laughable in the kitchen."

"As laughable as you are when you're pretending to be a birdbrain?" Trent said without batting an eye.

Lily's jaw dropped. She'd been found out. How could she explain to him that she thought that what she'd been doing was just as silly as he thought it was? It was getting too complicated. Better he should think her a fool than an idiot. She decided to deny the whole thing.

"I don't know what you're talking about."

"Come on, Lily, you know exactly what I'm talking about. I heard you laughing to yourself when you thought I was out of earshot. I wasn't. I was standing on the other side of the door wondering what would make a woman like you, a woman who seems to have at least half a brain in her head, act like a dimwit. I knew something was up, but the laugh tipped me off right away."

"I'm afraid I don't understand, Trent. It's a bit above my head." Lily rose as if to leave. "I'm very tired, and you're giving me a headache." But what she really meant was that she was giving herself a headache. "I think I'll go to bed now." She began to walk toward the stairs.

Trent leapt up and placed himself between her and the stairway. "Not until you admit that you've been putting on a big act since we got here." He stood in front of her adamantly.

"I haven't," Lily said simply. "Please get out of my way." She headed toward him.

"You have." He stretched out his arms to block her passage as she tried to sidle around him. "You've been pretending to be a dumb blonde because you thought that would turn me off, and you were right. It does. But you forgot something. I'm *not* dumb, and I know when my leg's being pulled. I find the whole episode rather flattering, though."

"Flattering?" Lily was at a loss to figure out why he felt flattered by her whole disgraceful show.

"Yes. You're afraid of me, of your feelings for me. That kiss we had outside wasn't like your average run-of-the-mill kiss, Lily; you know how it made you feel. You're afraid of your attraction toward me and mine toward you. You're frightened to be alone with me because it takes so much of your self-control to stay out of my arms."

He approached her slowly, as if she were a frightened animal, and wrapped her in his arms. Lily accepted his embrace willingly, as if his arms were the only, the right, the best place to be.

"Ah, Lily love, admit it." His violet eyes searched hers. "If I was your husband, it wouldn't be too distasteful." He kissed her lower lip, and then slowly, agonizingly, bit its full center, scraping the flesh tenderly between his teeth while his deep indigo eyes held hers captive, as if he were a hypnotist. "Does this frighten you?"

"No," Lily heard her own breathless voice answer as if from far away. Where had all her resistance gone?

He moved his hands down to massage her back while his lips trailed from her mouth to her neck, kissing a sensuous passage past her collarbone. Pushing aside the collar of her fur, he touched his lips against the silk that covered the cleavage between her breasts. The heat of his mouth burned through the soft fabric. With the utmost delicacy, he slipped her fur off her shoulders. His hands brushed gently at the fabric covering her breasts, and then, possessively, covered their ample mounds. He teased each nipple between his thumb and forefinger until they stood erect and sensitive to his touch.

"And now? Are you frightened now?" he asked, rubbing each nipple and sending sharp pinpricks of passionate sensation through every nerve of Lily's body.

"No." It was barely a whisper. Lily had all but lost control.

His lips found her mouth again, and he kissed her so deeply, so completely and so demandingly that she had no choice but to return the kiss in kind. Trent's hands uncovered her breasts, and he pressed her body tightly against his as he placed one hand beneath the fur at her back and the other on the tender flesh of her neck beneath her mane of tangled blonde hair, his thumb fondling the even tenderer flesh behind her ear. His tongue parted her lips and began slowly to explore her mouth, discovering erotic areas that Lily had never known existed. Their tongues entwined in a lascivious dance as the kiss built to a fever pitch.

Lily felt herself sinking deliciously into the most extravagant sensations. All she wanted was more of Trent. She couldn't press herself close enough against him. And then, suddenly, Trent was pulling away. She tried to pull him back, willing him to stay close and protective, but his will was stronger. He held her at arm's length.

"Do you need further proof, Lily?" he asked, his eyes flashing.

"Proof? I don't . . ." Lily mumbled, but her lips felt bruised and swollen, and she couldn't make them form the words. And her body was drowsy and languorous and still craved his touch.

"You want me. I know. But I can wait until *you* know and are willing to stop playing your silly games."

He turned to head up the stairs. But before he ascended, he touched her cheek briefly with his fingers. "Good night, Lily. Sweet dreams."

Lily stood as if she were already dreaming, watching him walk up the stairs. Part of her wanted to run after him and throw herself into his arms. But the other part, the proud and sensible part, kept her feet planted firmly on the ground.

3

Lily wasn't ready to go to bed yet, so she made herself a cup of coffee and sat in front of the window again. She hoped that looking out over the hills covered with snow beneath the smooth silver glow of the moon would stop the questions from forming in her mind. Questions like, How could she be so attracted to a man who obviously had no consideration for her feelings? Who couldn't resist teasing her constantly? And who seemed to take great pleasure in pricking her ego with his pointed barbs? He might want her, yes, but she was sure that he wanted her only in a physical way. He didn't seem to care at all for her herself. He disliked her writing, although he had never even read her books. And perhaps that was even worse; he had looked at her and decided right off the bat that her writing couldn't be of any consequence. And he seemed to think she was scatterbrained. Of course, she hadn't done much to change that opinion.

The chemistry between them had been volatile from the start. They seemed to grate against each other like a rusty saw cutting through a recalcitrant piece of wood. Unless they were kissing, and then Lily's very blood seemed to sing through her veins. Did his?

The moon shone down on the hills and the lake, and a single beam caught a corner of Lily's dress, turning the blue silk into silver. She had heard once that it was dangerous to sit in the moon's beam, that it could drive a person crazy, but she couldn't get much crazier than she already was—falling for a man whose words drove her to angry retaliation and whose kisses drove her to distraction.

She had been sitting too long with her thoughts and she wasn't making any headway with them. The world outside was peaceful and white, but inside she was in turmoil. She decided to explore the house, since she felt so restless. Perhaps activity would calm her nerves. She passed through the living room and into a hallway. Following the hallway, she came to a door, and, opening it, she found a set of steps that led down into what she supposed was the basement. But her nose detected the odor of chlorine. She flipped the light switch on the wall, completely unprepared for what she saw.

Before her was a large pool of blue water surrounded by plants and flowers of every description. Like the living room, this room had one whole wall made of glass that faced the same tranquil snow scene. Lily stepped down to the pool and knelt at its edge, dipping her hand in to test the temperature of the water. It was almost as warm as a bath. It would be nice to take a short dip, but she didn't have a bathing suit. Well, what did it matter? Trent had gone up to bed and was probably asleep by now. There was no one to see her if she decided to take off all her clothes and jump in for a quick swim, and the exercise would probably make her sleepy.

Lily stepped into the dressing alcove and removed her clothing quickly. She plucked a towel from a pile and placed it next to the pool. Then she poised on her toes and made a clean dive into the water. How wonderful it felt! She sliced through the water and reached the other side quickly. She swam back and forth with fast, sure strokes, and even did racing turns at the end of each lap. She was surprised that she could remember how to do them, since it had been so long since she'd practiced, but some things came naturally, and Lily had always felt completely comfortable in the water, as if it were her natural element. It felt wonderful to be doing something so effortlessly and without any of the self-consciousness she'd felt ever since she had met Trent that afternoon. She had reached the end of a lap and had somersaulted underwater to head back to the other end when the overhead lights went out. In their place the pool was lit up with deep blue and magenta underwater spots. What was going on?

"Practicing for the Olympics, Lily?"

It was Trent. He must have heard her splashing. Now she was trapped in the pool, stark naked. At least there were parts of the pool that were less lit up than others. She slowly swam over to one of the darker areas so her nakedness wouldn't be so visible.

"You're quite a good swimmer." His voice was deep and throaty. He walked over to where she was treading water and crouched at the edge of the pool.

"Keep your distance, Trent. I'm a pretty good splasher, too."

"You wouldn't splash *me*, would you?"

"I might, if you tried anything funny." Lily couldn't decide if she was scared or excited. She didn't know what he was going to do, only that he'd do the thing she least expected him to, and that she'd be completely unprepared.

"Lily, we have to talk about this idea you have that I'm always trying to do funny things to you." Trent's tone was halfway between serious and joking.

"It's not an 'idea,' it's the truth."

"What have I tried to do that's been funny?"

"Well . . ." How could Lily say what she wanted to say without seeming like a fool? That he tried to kiss her, and that she liked it when he did and then changed her mind afterward? That wasn't his fault, it was hers. "What about this idea you have about acting like we're really married?"

"I'm just trying to get into the part. Don't you know that's what actors do? They have to practice and imagine that they actually are whoever they're playing at being. I'm just doing my homework."

"Why don't you do your homework by yourself? Why don't you use your imagination?"

"Because I like kissing you, Lily." He said it simply. "And I think you like to kiss me, too." In the half-light of the pool, Lily could see the intensity of his gaze. His eyes were indigo again.

"Do you?" He was persistent. "Do you like to kiss me?"

"Why is it so important to you? This is just a job, isn't it? You're just doing it for the money, aren't you?" Lily's voice was thin and tight. She didn't know what she wanted him to say. Would she be relieved if he said yes, he *was* doing it for the money, or would she feel desolate? She was confused again, just as she always was whenever she was with Trent.

"Lily, come here." He stretched out his arm to where she was wearily treading water in the middle of the pool. He had said the words so simply and directly that she found herself responding to his request without any thought of questioning it.

"Yes?" She grasped the edge of the pool but kept most of her naked body beneath the surface of the water. She looked up at Trent and saw his eyes widen as he looked down at what he could see of her body in the jewel-like glow of the underwater lights. His hand reached out and cupped her wet face. It was warm and strong against her damp cheek. His thumb wiped away the remaining wetness on the crests of her cheekbones. His caress was strong and sure and thrilling as he leaned down and softly brushed his lips against hers.

"Ah, wet . . ." He intensified the kiss. He reached around to cup the back of her head so that he could press his mouth closer to hers. Lily could feel the tingles rushing down her spine. She was a willing captive of Trent's mouth. Finally he let her go.

"I've always wanted to kiss a mermaid," he said breathily.

Lily's own breath was coming in erratic bursts. She floated dreamily by the edge of the pool, her knuckles white with the effort of grasping the tile edge. The silence between them was deep and long until Trent broke it.

"Now, I'll ask you again. Do you like kissing me?"

"Yes. Yes, I do," Lily said fiercely. "I like to kiss you. Are you happy now?" Lily broke her grip on the edge of the pool and swam away furiously. He had to break their beautiful mood with his question! It was obvious that she liked to kiss him, and unless he was completely insensitive, he should know that. Hadn't he even said before that he knew she liked to? So why did he have to make her *say* it? It was all a matter of his damn ego. It wasn't enough for him to know that he could hold her captive with a kiss; he had to make her say it to his face. He had to have his power over her made completely and utterly clear to both of them so he could glory in it. She swam quietly now, hoping that if she ignored him he would go away.

"Lily?" Trent called her from across the pool.

"Please go away, Trent. You have your answer. What more could you want now?"

"I don't think you understand me."

"Trent, has it ever occurred to you that it really doesn't matter to me whether we understand each other or not? All I care about is the job we have to do. Now, I'd like to get out of the water. Would you please leave?"

"Not until we understand each other."

"Trent, I could stay in this pool until I shriveled up into a prune and we still wouldn't understand each other."

He laughed. "Well, maybe you're right, Lily. But I won't leave. I wouldn't miss the sight of your beautiful body rising from the water like some kind of goddess of the deep for anything in the world. Moments like this don't happen many times in a man's life, and I'm not about to pass this one up."

Lily laughed too. Trent was a master at knowing when

to make her laugh to ease the tension between them. "I'm afraid I'll look more like a drowned rat than a goddess of the deep."

"Well, I won't know unless I watch, will I?" He stood at the head of the pool, where the water shallowed, and crossed his arms over his chest, waiting. He wasn't joking.

"Trent, don't be silly. Give me my towel," Lily demanded.

"No," he replied obstinately.

"All right, you'll be sorry." Lily swam to the edge of the pool and splashed two big handfuls of water at Trent, soaking him from head to foot.

"You little devil!" he exclaimed, and as he was wiping the water out of his eyes, Lily jumped out of the water like a shot and grabbed her towel.

"Hey, give me some of that towel." He lunged toward her.

She sidestepped his grasp. "Say please."

"Please, Lily."

"No."

She ran around to the other side of the pool and watched him coming after her. Now she was teasing him. At last she had him at her mercy.

"All right. I'll just get another one."

"Oh." Lily hadn't thought of that. He had outsmarted her.

Trent reappeared from the dressing alcove with a towel and began to wipe himself dry. Lily walked slowly around the edge of the pool until she was standing a few feet away from him. He looked silly drying himself with all his clothes on.

"You're quite a handful, you know," he said wryly, looking at her with amusement.

"So are you." She felt so shy all of a sudden.

"Here. Your hair's all wet." He approached her and began ruffling her hair with his towel.

She stood quietly, reveling in being cared for. He rubbed her hair until most of its moisture was absorbed into the towel.

"There. All dry." His hands fell to his sides and he caught her eyes with his. "You're lovely, so lovely. . . ." He placed his hands on her shoulders and drew her slowly to him. "Why do you fight me so?"

Lily didn't know how to answer his question. Why *did* she fight him? Because he was arrogant? Because he teased her mercilessly? No, it was because he set off feelings in her that she'd never experienced before, and their newness and their intensity were frightening. She didn't want to give in to something so unknown. She didn't know how to act with him. She'd loved and trusted before, and what had happened? She'd been left behind. She could never let that happen again. She remained mute.

"Lily, tell me about James," Trent asked softly.

That was something Lily had been waiting for, and yet she had no ready response.

"He was someone I knew."

"Were you lovers?" Trent said the last word so softly that she wasn't sure if he had really said it. He was being kind, but he wanted to know.

"Yes." She turned away from him and pulled her towel tighter around her body, as if it could stop the hurt that was welling up within her.

"What happened?" Trent moved up behind her, and although he didn't touch her, she could feel his presence to the marrow of her bones.

"He . . ." Finally she had to say the words that she had been avoiding even thinking about. It was time to admit it. "He left me."

"Did you love him?"

Tears began to well in her eyes and Lily was helpless to stop them from coursing down her cheeks. "Yes . . . I did then, but now I don't know." Trent's question was confusing her. She had been so sure, at the time, that she had been in love with James. She couldn't have given herself to him so wholeheartedly if she hadn't. But now, under Trent's thoughtful gaze, she was beginning to realize that maybe she hadn't really loved him at all. She had wanted to be in love, and so, perhaps, she had convinced herself that she was.

"Lily, I'm sorry." Trent turned her around and gathered her in his arms. "I didn't mean to make you cry. I'm prying. Please forgive me."

She looked at him, but he was merely a blurred image through her tears.

Trent cupped her face with his hands. "He was a damn fool to leave you."

"Well . . ." Lily suddenly became nervous. She had exposed so much of herself to Trent in those few minutes, and she still didn't know whether or not she could trust him. What if he used what she had just told him against her? What if he began to tease her about James just as he had teased her about having to hire a husband? Oh, God, she had just set herself up again!

She pulled herself briskly out of his embrace. "I'm getting cold. I'm going to get dressed, and if you don't mind, I'd like to do that by myself. I doubt there's any chance I'll look like a goddess putting my clothes back on."

Trent looked at her sharply. "All right. I'll be in the kitchen making tea if you'd care for some."

"Okay." Lily had already moved into the alcove and was gathering up her clothes so that he'd understand completely that he was being dismissed.

Trent left quietly.

Lily put on her clothes quickly. The pool had been warm, but the air was cold, and she was breaking out in goose bumps. Trent's instinct had been right: She did want some hot tea. But did she want to drink it with him? Sometimes she felt as if he were some kind of pesky bug, buzzing around her and annoying her to no end. One minute he acted one way, and the next he acted another, and she never knew which it would be: the teasing, taunting Trent, or the Trent who could make her bones practically melt with his kisses and soft words and caresses.

Lily pulled on her stockings and attached them to her garter belt, then let her silk dress drop around her legs. She slipped her feet into her pumps, whose suede hadn't hardened as she'd feared. She picked up the towels she and Trent had used and hung them in the dressing room. Now she'd have to make up her mind about whether or not she'd go have tea with Trent. She supposed she could make one more stab at trying to get along, but . . . What was she thinking? It was impossible. Unfortunately, if she didn't go into the kitchen to have tea with him, he'd probably show up in her bedroom with a tray, insisting that he serve her in bed. And being served in bed by Trent was something she knew she should avoid. If his kisses could send fire through her veins even while her teeth were chattering in a snowstorm or while she was treading water in a pool, who knew what his kisses could do to her in bed? She blushed and was glad no one could see her flushed face. Now that the thought of Trent in her bed had crept into her mind, it was hard to force it back out again. She imagined his strong arms around her, his lean length pressed against her and his mouth against her lips. She touched her lips and they almost seemed to burn with the memory of his kisses. Her heart began to pound and a tingling began to move down her spine. How could she face him in such an agitated state?

She slipped off her shoes. She would try to sneak up to her room without him catching her; she was going to go to bed, and if he knocked, she wouldn't answer. She'd pretend she was asleep.

Slowly she padded up the stairs and, after opening the door, passed through into the hallway. With steps as soft as a cat's, she made it to the stairway, but the boards of the treads began to creak. Oh, no! She had forgotten how old boards could give one away. She heard a rustle of movement behind her.

"Tea, Lily?"

She turned slowly, like a thief caught in the act. "No, I don't think so. I'm just going to bed."

"Why are you always running away?" Trent stood below her, an adamant look on his face. "Can't we just sit and have tea like the two civilized human beings we are?"

"Civilized is not quite how I'd describe you, Trent," Lily answered sharply.

"Why? Do I slurp my soup? I assure you, Lily, my table manners are straight out of Emily Post."

"I'm sure they are. It's your other manners that I'm not quite sure of." Lily began to walk upstairs slowly. Go slowly and don't show fear, she was saying to herself, and maybe he'll leave you alone this time.

"Run away, Lily," Trent said softly. "You think you're running away from me, but you're really running from yourself."

Lily stopped and snapped, "Trent, you talk in riddles."

"Think about what I'm saying, Lily. You know it's true."

"I'm tired of your games, Trent." Lily spoke quietly, but with a hard edge to her voice. "You've been baiting me ever since we met this afternoon, and I'm sick to death of it."

"I've made myself perfectly clear."

She stopped and turned to face him. "I know. You hate my writing. You think I'm frivolous and shallow, and you don't allow a moment to pass without reminding me of it." Lily began to walk upstairs again.

Trent came up behind her swiftly and placed a hand on her arm to stop her.

"Let me go. Please."

"No. Not until I make myself perfectly clear."

"I've heard that promise before, but you *never* make yourself perfectly clear. You're as clear as mud, Trent."

"Give me one more chance and I promise you that I *will* make myself clear."

"All right." Lily sat down on the steps right where she was and wrapped her arms around her knees. She would give him one more chance. But that was all. "Shoot."

Trent obviously hadn't been expecting her acquiescence, and he seemed at a loss for words.

"I'm waiting." Lily tapped her toe impatiently against the stair.

"I don't hate your writing." That was all he said. As if that was all he needed to say.

"Of course you don't. You've never read it. You leapt to the conclusion that you hated it. You're just envious because I'm published and you're not."

Trent looked at her with widened eyes.

"You don't think," Lily continued, "that it's fair that I should have my books published, because it's obvious I don't need the money. You think I'm just a rich girl who fell into writing and never had to work hard to be published. But you've never seen me in the middle of the night working on one of my books, in a state because I'm not getting the dialogue right or my characters just don't seem to be coming alive on the page. You look at me and you think it's all fun and games, don't you?"

Trent looked up at her and he didn't need to say a word. The look in his eyes told her more than any words could have that she had hit the nail right on the head.

"You're right," he said slowly.

"Right," Lily answered briskly, and then rose to leave.

"Just a minute." Trent grabbed for her hand. "Now I get to say what *I* think is the truth. Turnabout's fair play, isn't it?"

Lily had a horrible trapped feeling. But she had to go along with his wish. Turnabout *was* fair play.

"Let's talk about why you run away from me." Trent pulled her down to sit next to him on the steps.

"All right." Lily turned to face him boldly. "Tell me, Dr. Daily, why do I run away?"

"You're attracted to me, and the possibility that it might be more than just a physical attraction scares you."

Did he think she was falling in love with him? His arrogance was amazing. "Oh, this is too much!" Lily stood up swiftly. But Trent had anticipated her movement, and he stood up, too, holding her close to him.

"Yes, it is too much. You deny it and deny it, but it won't go away."

"Trent, I've already fallen in love and it was a disaster. Do you think I'm going to do it again?"

"You weren't in love," he said with conviction.

"Who are you to say if I was or I wasn't? How would you know?"

"Because if a woman loves a man and he leaves her, she goes after him, she doesn't just accept it."

"If she has pride . . ."

"Love has no pride." He said it quietly, but it seemed to scream in Lily's mind because it was the truth. It had never occurred to her to go after James. She had just let him go because somewhere inside she must have known that she didn't really love him, or he didn't really love her, or . . . oh, her mind was a hopeless mess.

"Am I right?"

"What does it matter? It's over."

"It matters a hell of a lot to me. Just because you loved once—or thought you loved once—and you lost, you refuse to try again."

"And why should you care, Trent? Just how do you fit into the scheme of things?" Lily asked boldly.

"Because maybe I'm falling in love with you," he replied.

Lily's heart melted momentarily at what he said until she realized how he had qualified his statement.

"Maybe. Maybe, you say . . . and I'm supposed to throw all caution to the winds because you say maybe. . . . How selfish, how incredibly selfish you are. I don't even know you."

"You know me." Trent pulled her roughly to him.

"I don't—" But her protest was silenced by his demanding mouth. His lips covered hers and teased her mouth into opening. His arms gripped her and pressed her against him in a wild embrace. His lips demanded submission, and she succumbed. It was as if all her will had been drained and all that existed was a raw, instinctual response to his desire. She clung to him to keep her balance on the steep stairs. His lips left her mouth and began to travel across her soft cheek and up to her ear. He nibbled hungrily at her earlobe and whispered endearments while his hands moved down her back and to the front of her body, where they pressed against her softly curving stomach and then lower to massage the place where all desire begins and ends.

Lily was burning up in his embrace. Her body was a vast, burning desert, and her lips sought his again as if she were parched from thirst and he were a cool oasis stream. She drank in the sweetness of his kiss, but it wasn't enough; she wanted more. As if he sensed her need, his hand crept up beneath her hem and made a slow voyage up the smooth silk of her stocking until he reached the exposed flesh of her thigh. He pulled his mouth away just long enough to murmur, "Oh, an old-fashioned girl," and then returned to her mouth as his hand continued its voluptuous exploration. His hand burned, his mouth burned, they were blazing together like a fire gone out of control.

"You know me, you know me . . . don't you, Lily?" His lips murmured their incantation tantalizingly against hers.

"I know you, I know you . . ." Lily repeated his words,

hardly aware of their meaning. But the soft words that Trent had whispered had broken their silent spell of enchantment and her mind began to cool and clear. *Did* she know him? How could she know a man she had only met hours ago? All she knew was what he chose to show her. To all appearances he was sincere, but appearances could be deceiving; she was well aware of that. Hadn't James appeared to love her, and hadn't she appeared to love him? It was too soon; it was much too soon. Impulsiveness had always been Lily's downfall. Wasn't that how she had gotten into this crazy situation with Trent in the first place?

Her sanity had come back, and accompanying it came a formidable resolve. With all the strength she had, she pushed Trent away.

"No, this isn't the time. . . . It's too soon. . . . I can't." She stood there like a confused child.

Trent stood next to her, his breath coming in ragged bursts. "We're back to games, are we?" He put a hand under her chin and lifted her face up so that their eyes could meet. His eyes were black and hard and shone brittlely, like obsidian. "All right, Lily, two can play at this game. Go up and think about *this* in your cold little bed: I'll let you go this time, but the next time I won't. Because the next time won't happen unless you come to me and mean what you seem to promise with those hot kisses of yours. Until then it's strictly business between us. I won't be trifled with." He let her chin go with a snap of his wrist.

Lily began to climb up the stairs, mute and slow, as if she were a zombie. Trent stayed where he was, and although her back was to him, she could feel his gaze burning into her. She dared not turn around to meet it, because she knew what his gaze held. Trent thought she was a coward, and perhaps he was right.

She passed through the second-floor hallway and turned the knob of the first door she saw. She stepped in and saw her suitcase and a bed, its cover already turned down. Trent must have done it. She removed her clothes mechanically and then slid in between the sheets of her cold, cold bed. Sleep came and enfolded her like a damp, chilly blanket, and she dreamed of nothing all night but arid, frozen wastelands

4

Action," the director yelled.

Lily and Trent were snuggled together on a bearskin rug in front of the living room fireplace. The stylist had dressed Lily in a slinky black evening gown and thrown a hot pink marabou-feather boa around her neck. Fluff from the feathers kept floating up into her nose. Trent was wearing a tuxedo, with the black tie untied. They were supposed to look casual and relaxed, except that Trent was obviously irritated and Lily was almost cross-eyed from trying not to sneeze. This was their twenty-first take of the commercial, because instead of snuggling up close to each other, they both kept edging away so that by the end of each take they'd be on opposite sides of the rug, glowering at each other instead of nestling together lovingly in the center.

They'd started out with the best of intentions. By the time the van with Fountaine, the director and crew, and Lily's agent, Bev, had shown up, they had had their act down pat. They strolled to the front door hand in hand and welcomed everyone with big smiles. Trent never missed an opportunity to fondle Lily lovingly, and she kept gazing up at him with open adoration, calling him "Lawrence love" and "darling." But after an hour or so of the act it had begun to wear on Lily's nerves. It was ghastly to have to pretend to adore someone she really couldn't stand.

And then there were the things they were supposed to

say to each other for the commercial! Lily knew why they hadn't been shown the script before they began to shoot, and why the writer was nowhere to be seen. Whoever had written it must have feared for his life. It was that bad.

Suddenly Lily broke out of her daydream and noticed that Trent was looking at her with an obviously phony smile on his lips as he poured champagne into the glass she held in front of her. He had what seemed to be a desperate look in his eye. Her mind had been wandering. Had it wandered so far that she had missed her cue?

"Yes, darling, I'd loooove some," she cooed, just as she was supposed to.

"Cut!" the director roared.

Trent looked at her with a frankly disgusted expression.

The director came over to where she and Trent were lying on the rug and began to address her in the kind of voice that most people usually reserve for very young children.

"Lily, you can't say 'Yes, I'd love some' until he says, 'Care for some bubbly, darling?' It tends to confuse the audience," he drawled sarcastically. Tim Paige was thin and nervous and bald, as if he'd pulled out all of his hair during daily anxiety attacks.

"Let's try it again." He walked back to his perch near the camera. "Roll 'em," he yelled, and then waited for Lily and Trent to rearrange themselves on the rug.

Trent whispered softly in her ear, "I'll bet you a kiss you can't get it right this time."

"You're on!" Lily replied fiercely.

"Action!"

Trent poised the bottle of champagne over her glass. "Care for some more bubbly, darling?" he crooned.

"Yes, darling, I'd love some." Lily pressed her glass against his hand just as the script had told her to; then Trent began to pour champagne into her glass. Lily began her little speech.

"I'm Lily Lansden, and this is my husband, Lawrence." Lily paused so Trent could nod his head in greeting. As she looked toward him, though, she noticed that the level of champagne in her glass was getting awfully high.

"After a glorious night on the town, we love to return to our secluded country hideaway . . ." Champagne was beginning to drip over the sides of the glass. Trent was deliberately sabotaging the commercial so he'd win his bet.

"Why you . . ." Lily raised her glass and then dashed its contents into his face. He wasn't playing fair!

"Cut, cut, cut!" Paige shrieked hysterically, grasping at his bald pate for nonexistent hairs. "What is going on here?"

Trent was wiping his face free of champagne and trying to hide a big grin while Lily sulked.

"I can't say these lines," she protested. "This script is all wrong. If we're supposed to be in the country, why are we dressed in evening clothes? It doesn't make any sense."

"I'll have you know, Lily," Paige said, "that one of our top writers wrote this script and—"

Lily was just about to interrupt him and tell him that she didn't care if it had been written by a five-time Pulitzer Prize winner, it was still horrible, when Trent beat her to it.

"Even geniuses have bad days," he stated tactfully. "I suggest we take a break. My leg's about to fall asleep." He rose and rubbed at his leg while he offered a hand to Lily to help her up. But she shook her head and got up on her own.

Paige looked at them silently and then threw up his hands. "Take five, everyone," he called, and then wandered away, shaking his head and muttering something about artistic temperaments.

The crew began to bustle about them, and then Albert

Fountaine broke through. So far their interaction with him had been minimal, although he seemed to be the most reasonable member of the bunch, which was surprising, considering he was the one who was spending all the money.

He took Lily and Trent by their elbows and led them off the set. "You know, you're right, Lily; the script's all wrong for you."

She looked at him in surprise. Did he want to scrap the whole project? She couldn't blame him if he did. She and Trent, on camera, obviously weren't the loving couple he had hoped for.

"Come and sit down, you two." He motioned them over to some chairs that had been pushed in front of the picture window.

Lily and Trent sat down, and then Lily looked at Trent guiltily, waiting for the axe to drop.

Fountaine settled his generous bulk into a chair and gingerly crossed his legs while he ran a hand through his full brown beard. "When you splashed that champagne on Lawrence here, that was the first genuine emotion I saw between you two all day long." His brown eyes twinkled merrily. "You're not the lovey-dovey couple you're pretending to be"—he looked at them one at a time, frankly—"are you?"

Lily eyed Trent warily, wondering what Fountaine was getting at.

"You're a healthy, all-American couple. You get into your fights once in a while, and you enjoy them. And I enjoy *that!* What do you say we do something different? Now that I've met the both of you, I can see that our original concept was all wrong."

Lily looked at Trent and saw amusement in his eyes. She guessed that "healthy, all-American couple" wasn't exactly how he'd describe himself and Lily.

"Lily . . ." Fountaine leaned over toward her. "You're a writer. And, Lawrence"—he looked over toward Trent

—"you're married to a writer. What do you say to you two putting your heads together and coming up with something different? Have a nice dinner together. Work on it tonight. I'm sure you'll come up with something better than what we already have." He looked at them both. "What do you say?"

Great, it was just what Lily wanted to do—spend the whole night locked up in a room with Trent while they argued about a commercial neither one of them, at this point, even wanted to make. But what could Lily do but agree? She looked over at Trent. Obviously the idea appealed to him; he was grinning from ear to ear.

"I think it's a terrific idea." Trent leaned over and slapped Fountaine on the back as if they were old buddies. "If Lily can't come up with something, no one can." He winked at her.

She was trapped. She had to go along or seem difficult and temperamental.

"Of course, we'll pay you extra, Lily," Fountaine said.

"The money isn't the issue; it's just that I have no experience writing commercials," she said flimsily.

"Oh, come on, Lily. Aren't you always watching them and saying that you could do better? You know you say that all the time." Trent was being perfectly obnoxious.

"All right. I can do it. I'm not one to turn down a challenge." Lily summoned up a smile.

"Wonderful. While you're doing it, drink some champagne for inspiration." Fountaine patted them both on the back as he rose to leave. "Have fun, kids," he said, and then wandered off, leaving Lily and Trent alone.

Lily glared at Trent. "Now look at what you've gotten us into," she accused.

"I beg your pardon, Lily," he began, "but you're the one who didn't like the script."

"And you're the one who sabotaged that last take."

"Forgive me if I was so overcome by your beauty that I lost my head and forgot to stop pouring the champagne," he teased. "But that's water under the bridge now, my dear. We've got a job to do and we might as well get started. And then there's the small matter of that kiss. . . ."

"You're not going to try to collect on that bet, are you?" she asked him.

"Are you welching on it?" he countered, his eyes snapping with amusement.

"No," she retorted quickly. "You disqualified yourself when you tricked me. You didn't play fair."

Trent eyed her calmly. "Maybe you're right, Lily. Let's just forget about it, okay?"

Lily nodded in agreement and didn't say anything. But she was thinking to herself that she wished he had been at least a little more insistent about claiming his kiss. Perhaps he had finally lost interest.

Several hours and a bottle and a half of champagne later, Lily and Trent were still arguing over the script that should have been finished already. Every time Lily came up with an idea, Trent insisted that it was frivolous or shallow or not funny enough. Lily complained that Trent's ideas were too far above the head of the average television viewer and thus completely unsuitable for the task at hand. The champagne, which should have put them in a good mood, mysteriously had had just the opposite effect. Trent's mood was foul and Lily's wasn't much better.

Trent shook another cigarette out of the pack on the table, lit it, and blew out the match with a weary puff.

"If you smoke one more cigarette I'm going to scream," Lily said, letting her annoyance show. "You know, it's not only *your* lungs you're ruining."

The ashtray was overflowing, and the air was thick with the scent of tobacco in the tiny bedroom they had locked themselves into to "brainstorm," as Trent had called it. To Lily, it was more like head banging. Pieces of crumpled paper and broken pencils were strewn across the floor beneath the hovering cloud of smoke.

"I always smoke when I write. It helps me think," Trent responded, his voice on edge.

"If you want to call it that . . ." said Lily testily.

"Maybe you should try one too; maybe that's your problem," he taunted.

Lily didn't even bother to answer his ill-tempered challenge. She got up from the chair she had been sprawled in and headed over to the window to throw it open.

"What we need is some fresh air," she said.

"What we need are some fresh ideas," Trent muttered.

"I've given you numerous fresh ideas," Lily said. "You haven't liked one of them."

"You've been less than thrilled with all of mine," he countered.

They glared at each other. Then there was a knock on the door.

"Just what we need, an interruption." Trent jumped up and pulled the door open. It was Albert Fountaine with a tray of food.

"Thought you might need some nourishment to sustain you through all your hard work." He stood in the doorway hesitantly, Lily noticed, as if he had picked up the bad vibrations she and Trent were giving out and wasn't sure if he really wanted to get involved. She headed over to him.

"Thanks, Albert," she said graciously, and relieved him of the heavy tray. "That was very thoughtful of you." She hoped he wouldn't ask them how they were coming along.

"How are you two coming along?"

He would have to ask, she thought.

Lily looked at Trent guiltily, wondering if he was going to put up a good front and insist that they were doing fine, or tell the truth: that they had made no progress at all.

Fountaine broke the silence. "Trouble in paradise?" he quipped good-naturedly, as he sank his generous girth into a dainty lady's chair.

Lily busied herself with the tray, setting it down on a bureau top and shifting things around nervously. She wasn't going to be the one to break the bad news.

Trent flopped back down into his chair and puffed on his cigarette. "We've had a lot of ideas," he answered noncommittally.

Fountaine looked wordlessly from Lily to Trent, and then back again to Lily, who was now standing in front of the bureau, wringing her hands.

"Let's talk about it," Fountaine said brightly. "Maybe I can be of some help."

"Lawrence doesn't like any of the ideas I've had," she began, and then Trent interrupted.

"Lily doesn't like any of my ideas, either," he said to set the record straight.

"Hmmm," Fountaine murmured. "That *can* be a problem."

Now that they more or less had a mediator in their dispute, Lily decided to take advantage of the situation. "I think that since I'm the writer, Lawrence should agree with my suggestions. After all, I know what I'm doing." She shot Trent a quick look of victory. He couldn't disagree with her or he'd risk blowing his cover as her husband.

Fountaine pondered what she had said and then looked over at Trent. "You know, I'm afraid that I don't even know what you do for a living, Lawrence."

Lily and Trent both spoke up at once.

"He's a lawyer," said Lily.

"I'm a doctor," Trent said, his voice carrying over hers.

Fountaine looked confused.

"A doctor's lawyer," Trent added quickly, trying to smooth over their obvious gaffe. "Malpractice suits and things like that."

Fountaine watched them both with a level gaze. "Interesting," was all he said.

Lily caught Trent's eyes, and she jerked her eyebrow up ever so slightly and allowed her mouth to turn up a bit at the corners to convey her congratulations on his being able to think quickly enough to get them out of a tight spot. She was impressed by his quick wits and his ability to smooth over a testy situation. Saying he was a lawyer hadn't been that far off the mark. He was an expert at diplomacy . . . when he wanted to be.

"May I make a suggestion?" Fountaine finally said.

"Of course," Lily and Trent answered in unison. They were together on one point: they could use all the suggestions they could get.

"Since you two obviously have such a"—he paused to search for the right word—"stimulating relationship . . ." Lily thought that was a nice way of saying that they fought like cats and dogs. "Why don't you write the commercial as if you were in the middle of an argument? Maybe the only thing you can agree upon is that you both like my champagne." He sat there proudly.

"Albert," Lily said, "that's a wonderful idea!"

"Terrific," Trent echoed her sentiments.

"See, there's something you can agree on," Albert said with a smile, and then he rose from his chair.

"All right, children." Already Albert had taken on a fatherly role toward both of them, as if they were battling siblings who had to be appeased. "Have some dinner and then get back to work. It's nine o'clock now. It's only a sixty-second spot, so if you work quickly you can probably have it done before it's too late; and you won't have to worry about memorizing the lines, because you'll have written them yourselves." He went over to the door. "If there's any more trouble, just give me a yell. I'll be down in the living room."

"Thank you, Albert." Lily saw him to the door. "I think

you've solved our problem quite nicely." She looked over at Trent and felt a small twinge of goodwill toward him. Perhaps they could write the script now without any more of their bickering.

The door closed behind Fountaine, and Trent and Lily were once more alone in the tiny room. The open window had let out most of the smoke, leaving in its place the fresh crisp smell of newly fallen snow. Lily walked over to the window to draw it shut, passing by Trent on her way. Her leg accidentally brushed against his sprawled thigh and she felt a sharp shiver of desire run down her back. Or was the shivering from the cold air coming through the window? Lily wondered about that for a second or two, and then pulled the window shut with a determined slam.

"I suggest we eat." Trent jumped up and headed over to the tray that Fountaine had brought in. "I always think better on a full stomach."

Lily watched as he helped himself to the soup, which looked deliciously hearty, and chunks of crusty bread and creamy butter. The crew must have included an excellent cook. When he had finished serving himself and settled back in his chair, she helped herself, then sat down on the narrow bed she'd taken as her roost. They ate together in silence.

"Well, what do you think of Albert's idea?" Trent finally asked.

Lily nibbled at her bread and then answered, "I think it's a good one. Appropriate, too, under the circumstances."

"But what can we disagree about?"

"The possibilities are endless," Lily observed wryly. "We don't agree on much."

"Hmmm," Trent murmured. Obviously he already had something in mind. "How about if we set it up like this: We're just coming back from a party late at night and you say something like 'Weren't you spending just a little bit too much time with that pretty redhead?' See, you're jealous and—"

Lily jumped right in before he could go any further. "Why should I be jealous? I'm not the jealous type. Why should I care if you were talking to some flashy redhead?"

"Because you're married to me," he said firmly, his violet eyes snapping.

"If I were married to you, God forbid," Lily answered angrily, "I would *not* get all worked up about your talking to a redhead. You could talk to anyone you liked." Flustered, she repeated herself. "I'm not the jealous type."

"I'll remember that," Trent joked.

"I don't see why," Lily snapped back at him. "You'll have no use for the memory."

Trent jumped up and stood himself before Lily, towering over her. "Can't you be objective about this?" he demanded. "We have to get this script written before we can go to sleep tonight, and if you don't start acting like an adult instead of a spoiled child, we'll never get it done."

"I am not a spoiled child," Lily protested, furious.

"Then stop acting like one. I've had a perfectly good idea that we should base our disagreement on the fact that you're jealous of my talking to another woman. Let's take it from there."

"Why can't you be the one who's jealous of me for talking to another man?" she challenged.

"Because that's not funny."

"And my being jealous *is* funny? You're just using this commercial as an excuse to make fun of me, to make me look like a fool," Lily insisted.

"Don't you even understand why it's funny?" Trent asked in exasperation.

"Because making fun of a woman is always funny. It's a cheap joke," Lily answered heatedly.

"No, no, Lily, that's all wrong." Trent leaned over until his face was close to hers. Lily could see the tiny vein that ran up the side of his forehead throbbing angrily. "It's funny because it's ridiculous. Why should the much-published, successful, charming and stunningly beautiful Lily Lansden be jealous of any woman? Why should Lily Lansden be afraid of losing her man?"

"Oh . . ." Lily let out her breath in a quick puff as if she'd been punched in the stomach. It had only taken a few well-placed words of Trent's to remind her, quite clearly, about James and the fact that he had left her. She knew it had been a mistake to tell Trent about James. She had known he'd wait and bring it up at a time when it would hurt her. Now he had done it, but she really didn't want to believe it.

Trent straightened and ran his hands nervously through his hair. He must have realized his faux pas. "Lily, please forgive me. I didn't mean it that way."

"What other way could you have meant it, Trent?" she replied defensively, trying not to look into his eyes, but still feeling the intensity of his gaze. She didn't want to give him the satisfaction of knowing just how upset she'd been made by what he had said. "You know as well as I do that it's not ridiculous that a man should leave me. I've got firsthand experience of that." Lily jumped up, ran over to the window and flung it open. The cold air was bracing and cooled her hot, teary eyes.

"Lily . . ." Trent came up behind her and placed a hand on her shoulder. She quickly shrugged it off.

"Damn it, Lily, look at me!" He grabbed her by the arm and turned her toward him, his other hand cupping her chin and forcing her eyes to meet his.

"I didn't mean it the way it came out. I wasn't even thinking of . . ." He paused, and then said the name softly. "James. I was thinking that the reason why your jealousy would be so funny was because I can't imagine why any man would prefer anyone else to you. You're very special, Lily.'' He continued to gaze into her eyes as his thumb reached up to her mouth and brushed against her lower lip in a tentative, questioning way.

Lily felt the roughness of his skin against the softness of her lip and imagined what it would be like to feel that roughness against the rest of her. Would it make her aware of every inch of her flesh, just as his thumb against her mouth was making her aware of each tender crevice in her lip? She was imagining what it would be like to have each and every one of her nerve endings caressed by Trent's sensuous and capable hands, when Trent must have decided to end her wondering. He leaned down and caught her mouth with his. Lily's eyes closed, and then fluttered open momentarily to see Trent's black and sooty lashes lying in spiked crescents on the tender curve of his cheek. He was such a confusing mixture: rough and then tender, angry and then remorseful, thoughtless and then supremely sensitive. She couldn't decide which he really was—devil or angel.

He reached around to the back of her head and cupped it in a tender caress as he spread his fingers and combed them through her thick golden hair. She replied in kind, weaving her fingers through his silken coal black strands. Their mouths were way past the stage of tentative exploration as Trent darted his tongue in and out between her lips in a tantalizing dance. She pressed herself against him and felt the strong and constant response of his muscular thighs. Still clothed in the black evening gown whose material was so thin and delicate that it was almost as if she had no clothing on at all, she could feel the tender buds of her breasts tauten against his broad chest. All of her senses were being stimulated by the mere closeness of him, and her mind was reeling with the passionate promises that their present intimacy could only hint at. They were so close now that their bodies seemed to be of one mind and one motion, moving together with the rhythm of waves lapping against the sand of torrid tropical shores. Then a frigid breeze of air forced itself through the open window, and it was enough to bring Lily back to reality. Things between herself and Trent were going much too far, much too fast. She pulled away, but her lips let go of his reluctantly and her hands fell from his body as if there were invisible strings still tying her to him.

"It's cold; I think we should close the window." She tried to say it in a normal tone, but her desire made her voice throaty with passion.

Trent looked at her calmly, but his eyes were still burning with his arousal. He reached over and drew down the sash of the window. "Better?" he asked, his voice ragged.

"Yes," Lily said, and then moved slowly away from him, stepping lightly. Her legs felt jellylike. Trent remained standing at the window, gazing out at the snow as it shone beneath the bright full moon. Lily sat delicately on the bed, more shaken than she wanted to admit by the power of Trent's kiss.

Trent turned to her, and she could see that his expression was thoughtful, not angry, as she was afraid he might have been at her sudden withdrawal.

"Lily, you should never underestimate yourself. You're a beautiful, desirable woman, and you shouldn't let what happened in the past with someone who wasn't even worthy of you affect you now."

"I know, I know, but it's just too . . ."

"Soon?" Trent asked softly.

Lily nodded.

"You'll let me know when it's not too soon?" he asked, and his tone revealed his hope.

She nodded again in affirmation.

"Good." Trent seemed satisfied with her response. "Shall we get back to work?" He smiled at her, and his smile was warm and generous.

"Yes." Lily smiled back at him. "Let's go with the idea you had. It *could* be funny."

Trent grabbed a yellow pad and some pencils, pulled

his chair over to where she was sitting, and they got down to work.

Several hours later they were done. It was a wonderful script: funny, sharp and to the point. Lily knew Fountaine would love it.

She rose wearily to her feet. "Thank goodness we're done. I'm going to bed."

Trent looked up absentmindedly, still concentrating on the last line of dialogue in the tiny portable typewriter Fountaine had provided. "All right, Lily; I'm just going to retype this, and then I'll be in."

He'll be in? Lily wondered. What does he mean? Then she understood. "Oh, no, no . . ."

Trent looked up at her sharply. "We're married, aren't we?"

He had her there. "In a manner of speaking."

"And married people sleep together, don't they? Especially happily married people." He drove his point home sarcastically.

"Not these married people," Lily said firmly. Did he really expect to sleep in the same bed with her?

"Do you want to blow my cover? And besides, I already talked to Fountaine about it. We're getting that nice big bedroom in the corner." He smiled wickedly. "I already moved your suitcase."

She was trapped. There was no way of getting out of spending the night in the same bed as Trent. She blushed, and then her stomach did several flip-flops as she thought about what a man and a woman usually did when they were in the same bed together. Well, tonight was going to have to be the exception that proved the rule.

"Take your time with the typing, Trent. We want to make sure it's perfect for Albert," she said calmly.

"Oh, don't worry. I won't be long. I'm an ace typist."

Lily stuck her tongue out at him childishly and then

escaped from the room, slamming the door loudly. Once she was outside she leaned against it.

This was too much! She didn't know if she could trust herself in bed with Trent. What if he tried to . . . ? But he wouldn't. Hadn't he said that she was the one who had to tell him when she was ready? But what if she felt ready? That was even more frightening. She could defend herself, she knew, against Trent's desires. But what about her own?

Suddenly a door opened to the right of her and someone peeked out. "Lily?"

It was her agent, Bev. Good Lord, she hadn't had a chance to say more than a quick hello to her all day!

"Come in and talk to me," Bev whispered fiercely.

Lily walked down to Bev's room, entered, and then shut the door firmly behind her. Maybe she could convince Bev to let her sleep in her room. Then she could get up extra early and sneak into the bedroom she and Trent were supposed to share. But she'd have to be devious about it. She sensed that Bev was thinking of herself as a bit of a matchmaker in the situation.

Bev was wearing her glasses, and a manuscript lay open on her bed. She must have been reading it before she went to sleep. Lily walked over to the bed and plopped down on it.

"I'm exhausted," she said wearily as Bev sat down beside her.

"I would guess so. How did it go? Were you and 'Lawrence' "—Bev looked at her slyly—"able to work together?"

"It was a little rough for a while, but we buried the hatchet. I think we're going to sell a lot of wine for Albert Fountaine." She rubbed her eyes. They smarted from Trent's cigarette smoke and the late hour.

"That's the name of the game," Bev said. She took her glasses and placed them next to her on the bed. "You make a nice couple." She looked into Lily's eyes, but Lily kept her face impassive. She had guessed correctly. Bev *was* trying to matchmake.

"Strictly business, Bev. Don't get any ideas."

Bev made a wry face. "How did it go last night? Did you use my advice?"

Lily avoided her glance. "It was okay."

"You're holding out on me, Lil." Bev knew her well enough to guess that there was a lot more to the story than what Lily was actually saying.

"No, I'm not," Lily tried to meet her gaze defiantly, but she was so tired that all her defenses were down. She squirmed uneasily on the bed, while Bev tapped a pencil methodically on the manuscript. The tapping finally broke her reserve.

"All right. He's attractive, and I'm attracted." She flopped back onto the bed and let her wrist fall against her forehead, knowing that it made her look like a pining heroine. She had to let her hair down with someone, and it might as well be Bev.

"I knew it, I knew it." Bev was getting excited. "It's just what you need after—" Suddenly Bev stopped short.

"After James?" Lily sat up and looked at her accusingly.

"I know we made that deal never to mention his name again, Lily, and I'm sorry, but meeting Trent is just what you need." Bev said it firmly and primly, as if she were Lily's maiden aunt or an advice-to-the-lovelorn columnist.

"I said he was attractive and I was attracted, but I didn't say I was falling in love with him. He's difficult and demanding and arrogant. He gets on my nerves and all we do is fight." Lily listed Trent's bad qualities as if she had to use them to convince herself that she really didn't like him. But deep down inside, she knew it was quite the opposite.

"Sparks, that's what it is. Don't you know that all romances have sparks?"

"This is far from being a romance, Bev," Lily said dryly.

"It's just not one yet," Bev countered.

"Not ever," Lily replied firmly.

"Why?"

"We're incompatible. I'm the rich and famous mystery writer, and he's the poor and starving serious writer. It will never work."

"Oh." Bev mused for a moment. "So it's at the point where you're thinking long-term commitment, huh?" She smiled at Lily in a teasing kind of way.

"No, I'm not," Lily denied hotly. "I'm just making a hypothetical statement," she finished lamely.

"Why don't you consider a fling?" Bev prodded her. "He looks like excellent fling material to me."

"Why don't you fling with him, then?" Lily replied crossly.

"Have you forgotten? I'm happily married." She was. To a big bear of a man who worshiped her. "No, Lily, he's all yours. And if I were in your shoes, I wouldn't pass him up. I've never told you this before, but now seems as good a time as any: I never liked James. But Trent, I like."

Lily looked at her sharply. "Why didn't you like James?"

Bev pondered her question for a moment and then replied, "I can't say exactly why, except he didn't seem sincere to me somehow." She evaded Lily's eyes.

"Bev, we've known each other for a long time, and I know when you're holding back. Why don't you tell me what you're thinking?" Lily leaned forward. She'd always trusted Bev's judgment when it came to people. If she hadn't thought James was sincere, she was probably right.

"I just think . . ." Bev began, and then stopped. "Please don't take this personally, Lily," she pleaded. "But I think James was using you."

"No, I don't think that's true." Lily refuted what Bev

said angrily, but in the back of her mind she was considering it. When they went out together, hadn't she always paid because James lived off a trust fund and never seemed to have enough money? But she hadn't minded; she had plenty of money, and she was generous to everyone with it. James was no different from anyone else in that regard.

"Lily, what did James do for a living?" Bev asked, probing.

"Well . . ." For the life of her, Lily couldn't think of anything that he had done to make money. The job in California had been his first. "He didn't need to work; he had a trust fund."

"But it wasn't enough, was it?" Bev asked. "I think you provided him with the lifestyle he thought he deserved. Without you he would have just been someone who wanted to live richer than he actually could."

It was too much for Lily to think about right then. She closed her mind to it and postponed it to a later date, a trick that had always worked for Scarlett O'Hara. Now was the time to maneuver herself into staying overnight in Bev's room.

"I'm so tired, I don't think I can get up. I think I'll just fall asleep here." She closed her eyes and pretended to be drifting off to sleep, until Bev poked her in the side.

"Ow!" She sat up quickly.

"Lily Lansden, you're a coward," Bev said angrily.

"I don't know what you mean."

"You know as well as I do that you're supposed to be sleeping in the same room as Trent. You're supposed to be husband and wife, aren't you?"

"That's not it. I'm just so tired." Lily yawned and fell back on the bed.

"You have a bed to sleep in, Lily, and it isn't this one." Bev started to push her off. If Lily could have been objective about the situation, she would have laughed. She was like a sleepy cat being pushed off its favorite sleeping place and digging in its claws to stay put.

"Bev Simmons, you are being mean!" Lily sat up again and glowered at her agent. Why wouldn't Bev help her out?

"I'm protecting my client from doing something that could ruin a very nice deal I've set up for her." Bev stood up, grabbed Lily under the armpits and set her down on the carpet. "Now, march."

"You sound like a drill instructor," Lily grumbled as Bev pushed her toward the door.

"Then obey me like a good little soldier. Trent won't bite. And if he does, just bite back." Bev grinned at her lopsidedly.

Bev opened the door, and before she knew it, Lily was out in the hall and the door had closed behind her firmly and irrevocably. She was on her own now.

She walked down to the room that she and Trent were going to share. She opened the door and flicked on the light, but she didn't need light to tell her that the room was filled with flowers—their perfume was overwhelming. Bouquets of yellow and white roses were strewn about the room in sparkling crystal vases. Attached to one of the bouquets was a note. She tore it open impatiently and read it. "Sweet dreams to the happiest couple I know. Albert."

"Oh, this is the last straw!" Lily muttered to herself. Everyone was conspiring against her, pushing her into the arms of Trent Daily. She couldn't even trust her own body to keep her away from him. What was she going to do?

She sat there quietly and put what little she had left of her mind to work. There was only one thing she *could* do: get into bed with all her clothes on and feign sleep. A sleeping body was an unresponsive body.

She turned out the lights and slipped into bed. She closed her eyes and actually tried to go to sleep, but the sweet forgetfulness of slumber evaded her. Trent's face kept floating across the backs of her eyelids. His large violet eyes snapped with laughter and then burned with desire. A shock of black hair fell across his right eyebrow at a rakish angle, reminding her that he was devilishly attractive. She envisioned his mouth and the way his lips seemed to beckon to her just before he would lean down to kiss her. She pressed her fingers against her own lips, trying to tame their wild need to be kissed by him. And it was then that the door to the bedroom opened. Lily quickly stuck her hands back down under the covers and pressed her face further into the pillow.

The door closed, and she could hear Trent padding softly over to the bed.

"Lily? Are you awake?" he whispered softly.

She remained mute while she tried to relax the muscles of her body so she would appear to be asleep. She heard pieces of clothing drop to the floor. He was getting undressed. Was he getting into bed with her naked? She felt the mattress shift as he slipped beneath the covers. And then she felt his hand on her shoulder.

"Lily? Are you asleep?"

She mumbled nonsense syllables, as if she were deep in a dream, while electric shocks traveling down her spine told her that she was far from it. She prayed that he'd believe her ruse. .

"If you're not asleep, Lily, sweet dreams." He leaned over and kissed her exposed shoulder, his lips burning into her flesh. And then he curved himself against her, his body mimicking her own form, nestling against her so that they touched at hip and shoulder and calf. He threw his arm lightly around her waist.

It was sheer torture to be so close to him and have to remain rigid and senseless, like a cold marble statue. But if she softened even just an inch of her body to his touch, she knew that the rest would follow suit.

Lily lay there for what seemed like endless hours, not really sleeping and not really awake, until finally she fell into a deep, dreamless sleep. Exhaustion, finally, became her only ally against him.

5

~oooooooooooo~

Lily awoke in the morning to the sound of a tap on the door.

"Lily and Lawrence. Makeup's at six-thirty."

It was barely dawn. Lily sat up groggily, her muscles sore from sleeping in the same position all night. She looked at her watch and saw that she had half an hour to make herself presentable before she had to be downstairs. Trent still lay sleeping next to her, his arm caught between her waist and her lap. She eased herself out of bed slowly, not wanting him to awaken until she could safely reach the bathroom that opened off their room. And he didn't wake up; he merely rolled over and pulled the covers up to his chin in a childlike gesture.

On her way to the bathroom, Lily padded softly over to the window and drew the curtain aside. The gleaming snow was caught halfway between the waning moon and the rising sun, and it shone pearly gray across the hills and valleys that lay before her. If only life were as effortlessly beautiful . . . She thought about the day ahead of her. After they shot the commercial, all that would be left to do in Connecticut would be to pack up and leave. It occurred to her that it might be a long time before she saw Trent again, since she had no idea what Albert's plans for them were after the commercial was done. They would probably have to do some dubbing of their voices, but that wouldn't be until after the spot had been edited in the studio, and that could take consider-

79

able time. She might not see Trent for a while . . . unless she decided to see him. He had made it clear last night that whether or not they saw each other was totally up to her.

She rubbed a velvety rose petal between her fingers and inhaled its sweet scent. Roses were the loveliest of flowers, but even roses had thorns. She pricked her finger lightly on a thorny stem. Her feelings for Trent, she thought, were just like a rose, soft, tender and just blooming—and yet there were the thorns to consider. If only he weren't so defensive about her success or so adamantly critical of her books, and if only she weren't so fearful of the sharp new feelings he stirred within her. She sighed and looked over at his dark profile against the white pillowcase. Sleep made his face relaxed and vulnerable, and the sight of it tugged at her heart. She had better jump into the shower quickly before her will to resist him caved in.

Lily spent a long time in the shower, shampooing her hair and soaping her body with her favorite perfumed soap. She lathered her thighs until her skin felt silken smooth beneath the bubbles. Then she soaped her breasts and felt their soft peaks stiffen beneath her slippery fingers. Her body was infuriatingly sensitive this morning. She wondered what it would be like to feel Trent's strong body against hers, his hands exploring her supple flesh. . . . She felt a slowly building, unfamiliar ache between her legs. This has got to stop, Lily reprimanded herself. She turned the shower to cold, hoping that the shock of the icy water would bring her back to her senses, but its stabbing spray only excited her further. She jumped out and began to towel herself roughly, but the texture of the towel only provided additional stimulation. Lily collapsed onto the edge of the tub. What was she going to do if just thinking about Trent made her this excited?

After a few minutes she finally calmed down. She

cracked open the door and peeked out, and saw that Trent was still sleeping. So, quickly, with just a towel wrapped around her, she dragged her suitcase into the bathroom and then pulled out a simple jewel-neck sweater in gray and a black pleated skirt and put them on. She added a string of pearls around her neck and pearl studs in her ears. She and Trent had decided the night before that they would dress casually, since the premise of the commercial was that they were returning from a pleasant evening with their friends out in the country. She blow-dried her hair and then brushed it vigorously until it fell in simple waves about her face. She did without her usual makeup, since someone would do that for her downstairs, and then tiptoed out into the bedroom.

Lily nudged Trent on the shoulder. "Wake up; make-up's in fifteen minutes."

He opened one eye and gazed at her blearily. "Is it morning already?"

Lily nodded and then headed out the door. "See you downstairs," she threw over her shoulder.

When she got down to the first floor there were trays of coffee and doughnuts on a sideboard in the dining room. Lily grabbed a cruller and a cup of steaming coffee, and watched as the crew set the lights in place and scurried about moving furniture so it would be out of the camera's way.

A few minutes later someone touched her on the elbow. It was Albert Fountaine, looking bright-eyed and bushy-tailed. "I love the script. It's just what I wanted. You and Lawrence did a terrific job."

"Thanks, Albert. We owe it all to you."

"Don't be so modest. Ah, here's your better half." Albert gave her elbow a sharp squeeze as Trent came over to them. He looked haggard.

"Ready to go?" Fountaine asked cheerfully.

"Sure." Trent didn't look ready at all. He looked as if

he needed at least five more hours of sleep. The makeup girl was going to have to work a minor miracle to erase the dark circles under his eyes, Lily thought.

Fountaine looked at him quizzically, then quipped, "Thank God for makeup," and walked away.

Lily stood next to Trent uneasily. "Do you feel better than you look?" she joked, hoping to ease the tension.

"Not much," Trent replied, and ran a shaky hand through his black hair. "Sleeping chastely next to a desirable woman is not my idea of a fun evening."

Lily looked at him guiltily and then chastised herself. Why should she feel guilty for not getting more involved with Trent? Theirs was a business relationship, wasn't it? But Lily knew that it was rapidly becoming more than that, and the speed of her emotional involvement with him was unsettling. Like it or not, she did feel involved. But she'd have to think about that later. Right now the makeup girl was beckoning to her.

"Do you mind if I go first?" she asked Trent.

"No," he answered wearily. "She'll probably appreciate the practice before she tackles me."

"Poor Lawrence," Lily murmured as she brushed his hair back from his face. Was she teasing, or was she genuinely sympathetic?

Trent grabbed her hand and pressed it firmly against his cheek. "It's not sympathy I want, Lily." His clean-shaven cheek was firm and taut against the soft pads of her fingers, and his eyes were fiery. She looked at him quickly, shaken by the intensity of his gaze.

"You were pretending to be asleep last night," he said simply, and then pressed his lips into the tender cup of her palm and nuzzled suggestively.

Lily neither denied nor confirmed his suspicion. Instead she reminded him of their agreement. "You said that I could tell you when I was ready."

"I was a fool to say that." His lips had traveled from her palm to her wrist and now were trailing a string of nibbling kisses up the sensitive underside of her forearm.

Lily could see that some of the crew members had noticed Trent's erotic exploration of her arm, and she began to blush. Their expressions seemed to indicate that they found the scene charming, but Lily found it infuriating. Trent really knew how to play to a crowd.

She jerked her hand away and wordlessly left him where he was standing. She sat down in the makeup girl's chair. She'd had enough of Trent's nonsense for the morning.

An hour later they were all set to begin shooting the commercial. The special filters that turned day to night were on the cameras, and Trent and Lily had positioned themselves outside the front door of the house so they could enter as if they were returning from a party. Lily's teeth were chattering even though she was wrapped up in her fur. It seemed like hours until she finally heard Tim Paige roar, "Action," and they were finally in motion.

Trent opened the door for her and she passed through. As she entered, she could see that although the room would appear to be empty to the viewers who eventually watched the commercial, it was actually crammed full of equipment and crew members. Before she'd gotten involved in this project, Lily hadn't really understood just how hard it was not only to remember lines but to attempt to speak them naturally when you were being watched by a bunch of cynical pros. She'd put in her apprenticeship yesterday; today she was used to their gawking.

She shrugged impatiently as Trent slipped the fur off her shoulders. "You seemed awfully friendly with that red-headed what's her name," Lily began.

Trent took off his coat and threw it and her fur down onto a chair as they crossed from the foyer into the living room. "Meryl? Meryl Hayes?" he asked innocently.

"How interesting." Lily stood behind the couch, rubbing her fingers against the piping of the sofa's upholstery. "You know her name," she accused.

Trent had walked around to the other side of the couch

and was facing her. "People do tend to introduce themselves."

"Especially when their dresses are that low cut."

"She was wearing a turtleneck, Lily," he reminded her.

"A backless turtleneck." Lily placed her hands on her hips, while Trent turned to a bottle of champagne that was nestling in a cooler of ice.

"I didn't notice," he said as he began to wiggle the champagne cork with his thumbs.

"You were too busy looking into her eyes, Lawrence dear."

The cork popped, and Lily jumped slightly. "Champagne? Feeling guilty, darling?" she teased.

"Have you forgotten?" Trent grabbed two champagne flutes and began to pour the sparkling wine. "We met each other five years ago to the day." He passed her a glass.

"You remembered." Lily smiled happily, accepting the champagne.

"Of course." Trent tipped his glass toward her. "It was raining. Your eyelashes looked as if they were tipped with diamonds." He leaned his head back and closed his eyes, as if remembering how she had looked.

Lily stared across at him, aghast. "It was perfectly clear, and your eyes were bloodshot." She swirled the champagne around in the flute impatiently.

"Lily." Trent smiled, mustering all his charm into a dazzling grin. "Drink your champagne."

"I love champagne," Lily said as they both sipped blissfully, knowing that it didn't matter what the weather had been like. They had met and fallen in love, and that was all that mattered.

"And I love you, darling," said Trent.

"Cut!" Tim Paige yelled gleefully. At this point in the finished commercial, a slogan would flash across the screen: "When you can't agree on anything, agree on Fountaine Champagne, and then see what happens. . . ."

"Wonderful, wonderful," Tim Paige crooned as he ran up to Lily and gave her a big hug. "We got it all in one take!"

Lily looked down modestly. "It's easy when the lines are right."

Paige let her little gibe go by the wayside. "Let's set up for the final shot."

The last scene had them cuddled together on the sofa in front of a blazing fire. They quickly took their positions. Trent snaked his arm around Lily's shoulders and they arranged their champagne flutes in opposite hands.

"Action."

Trent looked up toward the ceiling, musing. "I could have sworn it was raining."

Lily looked at him fondly, as if excusing him, and all males, for their perpetual absentmindedness about the details of courtship.

"Cheers, darling." She clinked her glass against his.

"Cheers," Trent repeated, gazing at her like a man enraptured, and then leaned over and kissed her tenderly.

"Cut and wrap." Paige jumped up. "I can't get over it. You were perfect!"

Crew members ran up to Lily and Trent and slapped them on the back. Everyone was deliriously happy. After the agonies of the previous day's shoot, they could hardly believe that this one had gone so effortlessly.

"I love it; I love it; I love it!" Fountaine was hugging and kissing them both with abandon. "And here's how we'll start it. The screen will be dark black and we'll just flash a white title: 'Mystery writer Lily Lansden and her husband Lawrence—a happily married couple.' It makes it so slice-of-lifeish." Slice-of-life commercials were big that year.

Lily beamed at him happily. "That's just what it needs

to set it off. Oh, Albert, I'm so happy." She threw her arms around him and kissed him loudly.

"How about a kiss for your husband?" Trent broke in.

Lily was so elated that she grabbed Trent and gave him a big smack too. But the reaction she felt to that kiss was considerably warmer than what she'd experienced when she'd kissed Albert.

Tim Paige ran past them, juggling several bottles of champagne in his hands. "Party time!" he yelled, and began to fill up lots of little glasses and pass them around.

Paige shoved a glass of wine into her hands. "It's traditional, Lily. We always party after a shoot. Keeps those ulcers away." He danced past her and began to refill the glasses that were already emptying. It was only ten o'clock in the morning, but everyone seemed intent on getting as soused as possible.

Lily looked over at Trent. "Well," she said with a tilt of her head, "when in Rome . . ." and smiled at him. They had done a good job. It was time to celebrate.

Hours later the party was still going on, although most of it had relocated outside. People were tossing snowballs at each other and writhing in the snow, making deranged-looking snow angels. A small group was rolling enormous snowballs to make a tall, portly snowman that was beginning to take on more than a passing resemblance to Albert Fountaine. Someone had gathered twigs and pressed them into the bottom of the top ball to make a beard. Crew members frolicked in the snow as if they had all reverted to their childhoods. Lily had tied her hair back and changed into jeans, boots and a heavy sweater, and was helping Tim Paige fabricate a giant snow sculpture in the form of a magnum of champagne. Their ill will of the previous day had been forgotten. Everyone was happily intoxicated and stuffed from the sumptuous buffet the cook had laid out.

Lily was slapping a handful of snow onto the sculpture when Trent came up behind her, surprised her with a snowball down the back of her sweater, and then ran away.

"You . . . !" She laughed, chasing him over the crusty snow until she tackled him and pushed his face into a bank of cold, white flakes. "Gotcha!" she yelled gleefully.

Trent rolled over, grabbed her to him and planted a warm kiss on her lips. "I don't like your hair tied back," he said, and pulled the elastic from her ponytail.

Blonde waves fell around her face in a silken cloud, and as she leaned over Trent, it formed a curtain around their faces. He kissed her deeply, longingly, as if he couldn't get enough of her.

But Lily pulled away. She felt as if each kiss, each caress of Trent's was like a hand clutching her and pulling her into the depths of a swirling whirlpool whose swift currents would resist any attempts she made at freeing herself.

"Trent, I'm tired of this," she said softly.

"You're ready to give in, then?" He looked at her, knowing full well that she meant just the opposite.

"You were such a gentleman last night, saying that you'd wait until I was ready. But today all you're doing is trying to push me into something that I'm not certain I want."

"What is it you *do* want, Lily?" Trent asked in frustration. "Is it James? Are you thinking of James when you kiss me?"

Lily watched Trent as he sat up in the snow and brushed the flakes off his down jacket. She had never thought of James while Trent was kissing her, of that she was certain. She thought of no one and nothing but Trent and his overwhelming masculine power. No, Trent's kisses drove thoughts of anyone else completely out of her mind. But could she trust him enough to tell him that since she had met him, James had seemed to fade away in her mind, leaving only a faint, unsatisfying shadow of mistaken and misplaced love?

"James isn't the problem. I am," she admitted evasively, hoping that he wouldn't ask her to expound on that.

"And your problem is that you're afraid." She should have known that he would have all the answers. "You made a mistake once, and now you're going to spend the rest of your life punishing yourself for it." He stood up and shook more snow from his trousers. "Well, I'm glad I finally figured that out. I can't be wasting my time with someone who's afraid of life, Lily. There's too much to do and be to be afraid. Can't you see that? You've found success as a writer; when are you going to find it as a human being?"

Lily couldn't believe that Trent could be so cruel. Who was he to talk? He hadn't found any success as a writer, and his personal life couldn't be much better than hers. He wasn't attached to anyone, was he? Who was he to hand down judgments?

She lashed back at him. "You resent my success, Trent Daily. I knew that from the first time I met you. You're envious and jealous. For all I know, you could be turning my life upside down out of some spiteful urge because I'm successful and you're not." She was fighting dirty and she knew it, but she didn't care. Trent's record wasn't exactly clean either.

Trent threw back his head and let out an angry whoop of laughter. "If you want to know the truth, Lily, it's you who's the jealous one."

"Me? What do you have that I could possibly be jealous of?"

"My integrity as a writer." He spat the words out fiercely. "I haven't sold my soul to the marketplace and I never will. I'll make it, and I'll do it on my own terms."

Lily stood up swiftly and grabbed Trent by the arm to prevent him from stalking off before she could speak her mind. She whipped him around to face her.

"Listen to me, Trent Daily. I'm only going to tell you this one more time. I write what I do because I love it and

I'm good at it. I'm not going to stand for you playing these kinds of games with me, as if you're the holy, unapproachable artist and I'm the hack writer." By this time she was punching his chest with her clenched fist. "Understand?"

"Plainly." He gathered her fists in his hands, threw them back at her, and then stalked off, his shoes leaving deep, angry impressions in the snow.

Lily trembled, watching his back recede. She was so close to tears that she was afraid she was going to break down right in the middle of the snowy field in which she stood. Where did he get off saying the things he did? Hurtful, spiteful things that hit too close to the truth. Because Lily knew she *was* jealous of Trent, although not in the way he thought.

She remembered a time a few years earlier when she had temporarily grown weary of writing mysteries and had decided to write a "real" novel. It was slightly autobiographical and thus very close to her heart. She worked tirelessly on it, rewriting and rewriting certain passages until she was sure they shone with the light of truth and humanity. When it was done, she had given it to Bev with much fanfare. In the week that it had taken Bev to read it, Lily was elated. She knew that when Bev finally got back to her she wouldn't be able to say enough glorious things about the new book. It was torn from her soul, so how could it be anything less than powerful?

When she had finally faced Bev over the desk in her office, Bev had merely passed the manuscript silently across the blotter at her and said four words: "Stick to mysteries, Lily." She had never said anything about it again. Lily had been totally crushed by Bev's short dismissal of her effort. It was then that she knew that if she was destined to be a mystery writer, she was going to be the best damn mystery writer in the world. She had a soft spot, and Trent had blundered upon it.

* * *

Lily was sitting on the front porch steps when Bev came and sat down beside her.

"The commercial's wonderful," she said. "You and Trent work well together."

Lily turned and looked at her warily. Bev was always trying to get her into discussions about Trent, but Trent was the last person in the world she wanted to talk about right then. She said nothing.

"Are you still mad at me from last night?" Bev asked.

"No," Lily replied with a touch of coolness in her voice. "I'm not mad."

Bev looked at her, opened her mouth to say something, and then seemed to change her mind. Lily wondered what she was reluctant to say.

"Were you going to say something?" She turned to Bev. Normally when they were together, they chattered nonstop. Why was Bev so quiet?

"Lily, what has Trent said to you about his writing?"

"Only that he's never been published. He seems to think he's too good for it," Lily said heatedly. "Seems to like to think of himself as the artist-starving-in-the-garret type. Why do you ask?"

"I just thought you might have talked about it," Bev said.

"Writing is one of the things we definitely *do not* talk about," Lily said emphatically.

"Well, I just thought . . . since you're both writers you might talk about it," Bev went on.

"Not unless I want to be insulted." Lily's spirits were sinking dangerously low; she was still rankled from her last encounter with Trent and his little speech about artistic integrity. "Sometimes it seems like no one respects mysteries," she complained out loud.

"I respect them! The reviewers respect them!" Bev insisted.

Before she could stop herself, Lily blurted out, "But Trent doesn't!"

Bev gave her a long, cool glance. "That's it, isn't it? It's Trent. He's been giving you a hard time." Bev smiled.

"Why are you smiling? He's horrid about it." Lily was on the verge of tears.

"I'm going to tell you something that my grade school teacher said to me when the seven-year-old love of my life used to yank my hair and call me knock-knees. 'When a boy makes a point of seeming not to like you, he likes you.' Trent is wild about you, but he's defensive about your success and so he criticizes your books. Give him one to read and then see what he says."

"I can't believe he could be that juvenile," Lily protested.

"Now I'll tell you something my mom once said to me: 'Scratch a man and underneath you'll find a little boy.' He's just a little insecure because you're famous and he's not."

Lily looked at her in disbelief. "Trent insecure? You've got to be kidding! And besides, why should I care about Trent Daily's psychological shortcomings?"

Bev eyed her shrewdly. "I think you care a lot. I think you're falling in love."

"No, never; not with Trent," Lily flung back angrily.

"Well, you think about it." Bev rose to leave. "I think it's time to pack up and go home. Ride back with me and we'll talk about it some more."

"I think I'm supposed to ride back with Trent." Lily had been trying to avoid that thought. The thought of spending more time with him, alone, made her stomach flip-flop.

"Judging from the expression on your face, I take it you don't want to," Bev said.

"No, I don't." Lily paused, and then decided to plead her case. "Let me go back with you. I'll tell Albert and Trent that you and I have business to discuss. Will you back me up if he doesn't believe me?"

Lily watched Bev's face as she pondered her proposal.

She crossed her fingers and hoped for a favorable response.

"All right. I'll bail you out this time," Bev finally said. "But when we get back to New York, you're on your own."

Lily jumped up and hugged her. "Bev, you're a real pal!"

"There's a condition attached, though," Bev stated. "Let me give a copy of your latest book to Trent to read. I think you should give him a chance."

Lily agreed readily. She didn't think it would change anything, but if it meant that she could avoid an unpleasant car ride with Trent, it was an easy enough request to grant. "I'll go pack my things and be down in fifteen minutes," she threw over her shoulder as she scampered into the house.

She hadn't seen Trent for the last few hours. Maybe he had been rude enough to leave without her and she wouldn't even have to confront him. But when she opened the door to their room, she saw him standing in front of his luggage.

He looked up. "Hello, Lily. Packing time." He threw a pair of socks deftly into his suitcase.

Lily said nothing. She went over to her case and began to toss things carelessly into it. She and Trent had been arguing ever since they had met, and the thought of trading angry words with him again left her feeling cold and empty. Maybe it would be best just to ignore him.

She went into the bathroom to gather her toilet articles together, and when she returned to the bedroom, Trent was clicking shut the locks on his suitcase.

"I'm ready when you are," he said nonchalantly.

With her back to him, Lily busied herself with placing a tube of toothpaste in her shoe. "I'm going back with Bev."

"You're supposed to go back with me." Lily didn't

have to turn to see the expression on his face. His anger was evident in his voice.

"Bev wants to talk about business. . . ."

"It can't wait?" Trent asked impatiently.

Lily finally turned to confront him. "No." And before he had a chance to challenge her, she added, "If you don't believe me, you can ask her."

Trent eyed her suspiciously, but if he didn't believe her, he didn't say so. He crossed his arms over his chest. "I guess this is goodbye, then."

"I guess so," Lily said, and returned to her packing, rearranging things she had already rearranged at least twice.

"I owe you a nightgown," he said to her back.

So, he remembered the torn and dirtied bit of silk and lace they'd left on the road just two days ago. It seemed like such a long time since they'd been stuck in the snowstorm. So much had happened since then.

"No you don't; forget about it," Lily said coldly.

"I want to buy you a new one," he stated adamantly.

"Don't bother," Lily said sharply, and then snapped the locks of her suitcase in place. She turned to him. Now they were facing each other across the empty expanse of the bedroom, both standing straight and defiant.

"You won't give in, will you?" he asked softly.

"Give in to what?" Lily tried to hold her temper in check, but she knew she was about to lose control.

Something in the way she stood, or the look in her eyes, must have told Trent that he was better off not answering her question.

"Nothing. Goodbye, Lily," he said. For a few seconds he stood there silently, raking her body with his bold indigo eyes, as if to imprint her image on his mind for all the time that they would be apart.

Lily felt a chill creeping with cold icy fingers down her spine. All she had to do, she knew, was to go to him, and he'd wrap her in his strong, warm arms and chase the chill away. But at what price? Did she have to abandon her dignity for love? Was it love, or just a hot physical craving she felt whenever he was near? She just didn't know. She let him walk out of the room—and probably out of her life—without another word.

6

It was a Saturday night and Lily was alone in her penthouse. Since she'd returned from Connecticut two weeks ago, she'd done nothing but seclude herself from the rest of the world. She told herself it was only because she was working on a new book, and that she always locked herself away for the first few chapters, but she knew the reason had to be something else. The writing was going horribly. Every sentence seemed dead on arrival, her characters all meanspirited and nasty, and the plot lifeless and contrived. She'd thrown out at least three times as much as she'd kept, which gave her a grand total of twenty pages that she could only consider slightly better than abysmal. Her nerves were gone; her weight had dropped by five pounds; her eyes were red and surrounded by enormous dark circles, and her hair was limp and raggedy. She couldn't stand to look at herself in the mirror anymore, and she almost prayed that she'd been stricken with some kind of dread disease to justify her listlessness and lack of spirits, but unfortunately she was as healthy as a horse and always had been.

Virtually the only person she'd talked to since she had returned was Bev, who had told her that she had given Trent one of Lily's books and that he'd brought it back without comment. Not exactly encouraging news.

She sat in front of her typewriter, gazing at a piece of paper that had remained blank for the past several hours. Now she was reduced from writing garbage to writing nothing at all. She looked around her, hoping that the room she had so carefully put together to write in would cheer her as it usually did, but the soft gray carpeting only depressed her spirits, and the bright, primary-colored throw pillows strewn across the beige sofa seemed agitated and askew.

Lily left her desk and walked over to the picture window that stretched from one end of the room to the other. Beneath her the stone canyons of Manhattan stretched endlessly. Twinkling diamond streetlights and the rubylike taillights of cars and buses formed an endlessly changing pattern in the chill wintry evening. She wondered how it was possible to be living in the most exciting city in the world and yet feel so dull and lifeless. She was acting like a lovelorn sap just because Trent Daily hadn't called. Well, so what if Trent didn't like her books? She liked them, and Bev liked them, and half a million people couldn't be wrong. Damn Trent Daily! What did he know?

She slammed her fist against the plate glass of the window. It was the first sign of spirit she'd shown in days, and it felt good. She looked at the clock on the wall. It was only ten, and in New York the night was still young. She could get dressed and go out for dinner. She hadn't eaten a decent meal in at least a week. And then perhaps she could visit some of her friends. She'd been turning down their invitations ever since she'd come back to town.

She was headed into the bathroom to draw a bath when the phone rang. Her heart leapt. Maybe it was Trent, although every time the phone had rung before she had thought the same thing, and it never had been he. She let it ring three times and then nervously picked it up.

"Hello?"

"Congratulations to the new bride."

She knew the voice immediately, even through the long-distance crackle. It was James.

"Thank you." She didn't know what else to say. She

couldn't tell him that she was just as single as when he had left her. Even if it *was* the truth, she didn't want to give him the satisfaction of knowing it.

"I'd always thought I was going to be the lucky guy," James said. His voice sounded oily. Funny, Lily had never noticed that before. It set her on edge.

"You should have told me," she said.

"Ah, Lily." He laughed too easily. "Still as sharp-tongued as ever."

"How is Los Angeles, James?" she asked bluntly to change the subject.

"Sunshine, cars and girls," he replied arrogantly. Especially girls, Lily wanted to complete the sentence for him.

"That's nice," she answered coolly.

"But really, Lily, I thought you were going to marry me," he said, pursuing the subject.

And then it hit Lily. How did he know that she was supposedly married?

"How did you find out?"

"Saw it in the trades, love."

Lily remembered now. Fountaine had had press releases sent out to the usual papers and magazines that handled news from the advertising agencies.

"Read all about your contract. What a coup for you and . . . Lawrence, isn't it?"

"Yes, Lawrence." What was he getting at?

"You know, Lily . . ." His voice lowered and became wheedling. "The job should have been mine. All you had to do was ask, instead of going off and marrying some stranger. You *are* married, aren't you? I mean, it's quite a coincidence, his last name being Lansden, too."

Was it a stab in the dark, or had he discovered her ruse? She decided to play dumb. "I'll send you a copy of our marriage certificate."

"Don't get so testy, Lily. I'm just asking. I don't like being cheated out of my just rewards."

"Just rewards! As I recall, James, *you* left *me*."

"I'd prefer to think of it as an extended vacation," he said arrogantly.

"Then you should have told me you'd be back when you left."

"No time, dear heart; they needed me here immediately." His reply was too easy and too quick.

"What *are* you doing out there, James?" Now Lily was curious.

"A little bit of this, a little bit of that," he answered evasively. "A lot of pining for you," he whispered across the long-distance lines.

Lily wanted to drop the phone; it felt soiled from James's greasy voice.

"That's nonsense, James."

"But, Lily, think of all the fun we could have with that money. . . ."

At last he got to the point, Lily realized. He didn't miss her, he missed her money—his meal ticket. Things must not have worked out on the West Coast. Maybe he had left her for another, wealthier woman and she had dropped him. The possibilities were endless, and all of them were distasteful. Bev had been right about him. He was a leech, and now there must not be anyone for him to bleed.

"I have to go, James; I'm going out. Thank you for calling. Your concern means a lot to me," she finished sarcastically. She would never tell him what she suspected.

"But I'm not through."

"I am." Lily slammed the phone down and then collapsed on the couch. She had her proof now—James had never loved her, only her status and her money and all the things she could do for him. But instead of feeling crushed by her new knowledge, she felt a strange sense of freedom. She had stopped caring for James weeks ago, so the final knowledge that he had never truly loved her had lost its power to hurt. But, since then, she had still wondered about why he had left. Now it seemed obvious

—he had thought there were better pickings elsewhere. To know the truth set her free from all her wondering about whether or not their breakup had been her fault. How could she ever have thought him worthy of her love?

Something in her mind clicked. Hadn't someone said something like that to her just recently? And then she knew who it was—Trent. Suddenly she was filled with a deep longing for him. She remembered how it felt to have his strong hands caress her skin, how his lips set off flames within her when he touched them to her own, how his eyes changed from deep violet to dark indigo when he was aroused, and how tender, how infinitely tender he could be.

But what about his returning her book to Bev without saying a word? Well, that could be because he had liked it and was too embarrassed to admit it after all the critical things he'd said about her writing. Lily's heart leapt in her chest. Bev had said he was wild about her, and maybe Bev was right. She thought back. Had Bev ever been wrong? No, no! Lily jumped up and began to spin around. He was wild about her, and she was wild about him. It was so simple. The differences could be worked out.

She decided to take a bath and then call him. She ran to the bathroom and turned the faucets on. No, she'd call him and then take a bath; she didn't want to waste a minute more. She closed the bathroom door to shut off the noise of the water tumbling into the tub.

Lily ran into the living room and picked up the phone book. She ran a nervous finger down the columns of Dailys. There were so many; what if there was more than one Trent? But there wasn't. She found his number and punched it out impatiently. It rang three times and then there was an answer. Lily was about to say hello when she realized that she had gotten Trent's answering machine and not Trent. He wasn't home.

She listened to the recorded message, and then, after

the beep, became tongue-tied. She didn't know what to say. She could ask him to call her, just cut and dried and businesslike, but somehow that didn't seem right. She pondered her choices until the tape ran out and the machine clicked off. Lily was about to hang up the phone when her downstairs buzzer rang.

She ran to the intercom and pressed the LISTEN button.

"Miss Lansden?" The soft Spanish accent meant it was her doorman, Adolfo.

"Yes?"

"There's a gentleman here to see you. A Mr. Daily. Can I send him up?"

Lily was practically struck dumb. Trent had come to see her! She managed to get out a quick and breathless yes, and then released the button.

She looked down at what she was wearing—her usual writing outfit of sweatpants, sneakers and a sweatshirt. Her hair was in a long braid down her back because she'd been too lazy to wash it that morning, and she had no makeup on at all. Not exactly glamorous; hell, not even mildly attractive.

She ran to her bedroom and began to rummage frantically through her closet; then she ran over to her drawers to pull out some lingerie. A moment later she ran back to her closet and scrambled around on the floor for shoes. She was standing wild-eyed in the middle of the room, an oxford in one hand and a silk slip in the other, when the doorbell rang. No time to change! She threw the shoe and the slip down into the closet, slammed it shut and ran for the door. But before she opened it she gave herself ten seconds to calm down. She was as nervous as a cat, but by the time she opened the door she had managed to fool herself into thinking that she was as cool as a cucumber.

She opened the door calmly. "Hello, Trent."

He looked even worse than she did, if that were possible. His black hair was spiky, as if he'd spent weeks raking his fingers through it. His eyes were bright and hard as if with fever, and his clothes were rumpled and mismatched. Beneath his arm was a box from one of the most expensive stores in New York. He held it out to her wordlessly.

She took it into her hands silently and then invited him in. He walked over to the couch and sat uneasily on its edge.

"I told you I'd replace that nightgown of yours," he finally said.

"It really wasn't necessary, but that's sweet of you," Lily replied, trying to keep her voice even.

"Open it," he commanded. His eyes were deep indigo.

Lily pulled the top off the box, and nestled beneath layers of crisp tissue she found the loveliest nightgown she had ever seen. It was gossamer-thin silk in a heavenly shade of peach. Its edges were trimmed with intricately worked ecru lace.

"It's lovely. It's the loveliest thing . . ." She ran her fingers across the silk. It was like being able to touch a moonbeam or fine silken sand or . . . or running her fingers through Trent's own fine black hair. The feel of it was exquisitely sensual. And the color was like the flesh of a freshly bitten peach—soft and almost juicy looking.

"I thought with your hair and eyes . . ." Trent's sentence trailed off as he rose and came to her side.

"I've missed you, Trent," Lily said simply. She knew she had to be the one to break down the walls between them. After all, she had been the one who had put them up.

"I've missed you, too," he answered as his eyes caressed her eagerly, lovingly.

"I don't think I've been fair to you," Lily began. "I've been defensive and childish—" She would have gone on, but Trent interrupted her.

"I'm the one who's been childish." He took her hand and led her over to the couch. "I have a confession to make."

Lily sat on the couch and let him envelop her fine-boned hand in his broad, warm palm. It felt safe and secure there. How could she ever have mistrusted him?

"What is it?"

"I read one of your books." His eyes were downcast, and then they lifted to meet hers. They were as dark and shiny as two luscious grapes. "It was clever and fascinating. I couldn't put it down. I don't know how you do it." He leaned over and brushed a stray wisp of hair away from her cheek. "You're a wonderful writer."

She knew that it shouldn't matter so much that this one man should think she was a good writer, but it did. It made all the difference in the world because, Lily was finally able to admit to herself, she was falling in love with him, and a woman always wants to please the man she loves.

Trent touched her cheek. "Remember that truce we made?"

"Yes," Lily whispered breathlessly.

"Can we make it again?" But he didn't wait for her reply.

He simply kissed her, and Lily felt her entire being melting into his hot embrace. His tongue parted her lips softly and then claimed her mouth, and their tongues lapped and entwined as the kiss intensified. Lily felt her throat tighten and her chest ache, and she was pierced by a pang of desire so sharp and furious that she almost felt faint. She clung to him like a shipwrecked soul in a storm-tossed sea, pressing her soft body against his hard muscled frame and feeling the tender nipples of her breasts tauten against his chest. Storm-tossed sea, crashing waves, water all around her . . .

"Oh, no!" Lily jumped up like a flash of lightning and ran toward the bathroom. No wonder she had been thinking of water; she had forgotten to turn the bathtub faucet off! The bathroom must be flooded by now.

She sped into the bathroom just in the nick of time. The water had just reached the lip of the tub and was beginning to cascade down the side. She turned off the faucets quickly and then waded across the quarter inch of water that lay on top of the tiles. She grabbed towels from the rack and began to throw them on the floor to soak up the spill. She looked up to see Trent standing in the doorway, his lanky frame completely filling the opening. He was laughing.

"I've never been stopped in the middle of a kiss by a flood before," he said wryly. "There's never a dull moment with you, Lily."

Lily was down on her hands and knees, swabbing like a demon and then wringing out the soaking wet towels in the bathroom sink.

"I was about to take a bath when you buzzed, and then it slipped my mind."

Trent got on his hands and knees next to her and swabbed too. "I've never given anyone temporary amnesia before, either." He leaned over and gave her a quick but probing kiss. "It's kind of flattering."

Lily rested her hand on the floor and leaned into his kiss like a cat stretching out toward its master's stroking hand, and then she felt her fingers slide out from under her on the slippery tile. She fell face first onto the floor.

"Yoooowwww!" Her nose was the first part of her body to make contact.

"Lily!" Trent exclaimed, and pulled her up like a limp rag doll. "Does it hurt?"

"Of course it does!" She rubbed her nose gingerly, trying to find the place where it hurt the most. "Ooow." She had found it. "Do you think it's broken?" she asked him.

He touched her nose lightly with his fingers. "I don't think so," he said. "But it's a little too soon to tell."

"Well, when will we know?" Lily asked impatiently. Now that the pain was subsiding slightly, she could allow herself to feel like the total fool she was. Imagine, breaking your nose right in the middle of a seduction scene!

"If you wake up tomorrow and instead of a nose you have a big red balloon, then we'll know it's broken," Trent replied with a straight face.

"Oh, wonderful," Lily said sarcastically. So they were back to teasing.

"But I'll still think you're beautiful," Trent said softly, and continued to caress her nose. It was almost as if his hands had the power to heal, because it was actually feeling much better. He kissed the bridge of her nose lightly.

"A broken nose always adds character to a face," he said.

"I think I have quite enough character, thank you very much," Lily said, and rose to her feet. She was drenched from head to toe, and so was Trent.

"I think I'd better change." She was beginning to feel cold and clammy and chilled. She must look a fright in her drenched sweatpants and sweatshirt, not exactly the kind of woman a man would want to make wild and passionate love to. She was surprised at herself. Was that what she wanted Trent to do?

"May I make a suggestion?" Trent's eyes snapped wickedly.

"Sure." His brilliant gaze sent a shiver down her spine.

"Change into my present. I'd like to see how it looks"—his eyes made a quick foray up and down her body—"in the flesh."

The tension between them was becoming almost unbearable, and Lily knew that it could have only one possible resolution. "And what about you?" she asked.

"I'll wear a sheet," he said simply, as if it were obvious.

"Oh," Lily said, feeling like an idiot. She was wildly considering what Trent's long hard body would look like beneath a crisp white sheet. It was slightly mind boggling.

He placed himself in front of her, put his hands on her shoulders, and then turned her around so she was headed out the door. "The nightgown's that way," he said, and then tapped her lightly on the fanny to get her moving. "I'll meet you in the bedroom."

Lily almost asked him how he knew where the bedroom was, but she decided that if he didn't know, he'd find it soon enough. Trent was like that—resourceful.

She wandered into the living room, took the nightgown out of its box and laid it on the back of the couch. Then she peeled off her wet clothes.

"This is certainly different," she mumbled to herself. "I've got a rendezvous with a stark-naked man in my bedroom. No time-wasting preliminaries here."

She pulled the nightgown over her head and sighed as its soft folds caressed her slightly damp body. How wonderful it felt! And how wonderful she felt. If she had thought once before that she was in love, she knew now that it hadn't been true. The feelings she had for Trent were completely different from those she had had for James. What her mother had always told her was true. When you met the right man, you knew it. It was as plain as the slightly swollen nose on her face. She was in love with Trent Daily.

She padded down to the bedroom and pushed open the door nervously. Trent was lying in her bed, propped up on a pillow, the sheet just covering him from the waist down. The sight of his naked torso sent a quick thrill through her body. He was a gloriously masculine man. He looked at her and raised his right eyebrow in approval.

"Turn," he commanded.

Lily stood on the balls of her feet and whirled. The silk billowed out and then fell against her curves, showing them off to perfection when she stopped.

"Ah . . ." He let out a sharp sigh of delight. "Better than I thought." He lifted his arm and motioned to her. "Come here, Lily."

She approached him as if she were in a dream. The light in the room was soft and diffuse. There was no need for the traditional accoutrements of romance, like roses or candlelight or soft violins playing in the background, when a man was as supremely sexual as Trent Daily. It would be like adding whipped cream to an already deliciously frosted cake.

She knelt on the bed, and then Trent swept the sheet aside. Lily almost gasped at what he revealed. His arousal was obviously as great as her own. Lily's eyes traveled up his lightly thatched chest and then met his own eyes, burning like volcanic fires. Gently he pulled her onto the bed and laid her down beside him. Even more gently he grasped the silky gown and tugged it over her acquiescent body, and then stopped as if awestruck to admire the riches he had just uncovered.

Her body stretched the length of the bed, a beautiful ivory woman crowned with a golden halo of luxurious hair and, nestled between her legs, touched with what appeared to be golden flames licking at her thighs. He sighed and pulled her close to him.

"Ah, Lily, you're so much more than I had ever dreamt you could be." He nuzzled his lips against her ear as he whispered endearments. "So beautiful, so lovely . . ."

He nibbled tenderly at her earlobe and then softly bit the fleshiest part. Wild tingles electrified every nerve in her body. Softly he began to caress her face and then her hair, and then his hand began to wander down the length of her body, exploring and exciting places that until that moment had been completely unknown to her.

Lily responded in kind, hardly knowing what she was doing or why she was doing it. It seemed as if she knew exactly how to excite Trent; he sighed and moaned her name over and over again. They began to move together in a primitive rhythm that only they shared, melting and melding together until it was impossible to tell where she began and Trent left off. Lily was lost in the most exquisite of sensations.

Their mouths were hot and almost greedy, as if they

couldn't kiss deeply or fiercely enough. And then Trent's lips left hers and began a tender voyage down her neck, leaving blazing imprints as he traveled to the soft mounds of her breasts and took one of their hard peaks into his mouth and gently, insistently, caressed it with his tongue until she thought she'd go mad with the sensations he was arousing within her. But he wasn't through. Across her softly rounded belly his lips nipped and then soothed the inflamed flesh until finally they rested on the sensitive spot between her thighs. And then his tongue began to dart and flicker like a fire gone out of control. Lily pressed her hands against his head and writhed in ecstasy. Wild white fire coursed through her veins and finally exploded in one grand eruption of ultimate sensation. A slow warmth bathed her entire body, and a feeling of pure and complete contentment gripped her heart. But Trent had only just begun.

He pulled himself up and then pressed himself against her. At the insistent nudge of his knees between her thighs, she opened to him and then he entered her with a hard, needful thrust. He began to excite her again, to build on the warmth spreading through her body as if he were adding kindling to embers. And now she was so perfectly attuned to him that her pleasure was even more intense.

Her pleasure was so exquisite and his need for her so commanding that she thrust against him repeatedly as if she couldn't be possessed deeply enough. And then his answering thrusts began to excite her to a frenzy. She climbed the peak again with him, and then, just as she was about to fall, he pulled her close and with one final forceful stroke he went over the edge with her as they tumbled together down the sweet slopes of desire, holding fast to one another as if they were the only two people left in the world.

Later they lay entwined together as the hot passion they had stirred and then appeased settled into a deep and true contentment. Trent still caressed her languorously, his fingers tickling teasingly down her thighs and across the tender flesh of her sides.

"How's your nose?" was the first thing he said.

Lily laughed throatily. "What a romantic question!"

Trent propped himself up on his elbow and continued to caress the soft curve of her belly. "Well, I know the rest of you is happy."

"Deliriously happy," she responded, and brushed his black hair out of his deep indigo eyes.

"Me too." He nuzzled his lips against the soft flesh of her neck.

"Trent?"

"Yes?" he said, nipping at her earlobe.

"Why are you called Trent?"

"I knew this would have to come up sooner or later." He laughed and sat up. "I was named after Trenton, New Jersey, where, my mother insists, I was conceived."

"Trenton, New Jersey!" Like most New Yorkers, Lily had a single-minded, and undoubtedly mistaken, vision of New Jersey as a vast wasteland of factories spewing sulfurous fumes into the air.

"Not exactly the most romantic place in the world. My father and mother were on their way to Princeton, where he was a visiting lecturer, had car trouble, and stayed overnight. Apparently they found Trenton wildly sexy." He laughed.

"I find Trent wildly sexy," Lily said ingenuously, giving his stomach a sharp slap.

"You do, you little vixen? How sexy? Show me." He pulled her to him roughly.

"Like this," she said, and then proceeded to show him just how sexy he was. Again they made their passionate exploration until the sun began to rise, and then, wrapped in each other's arms, they fell asleep.

When Lily awoke late the next morning Trent was gone. Groggily, she wondered if last night had been a dream, but then she noticed that the pillow next to hers still held the imprint of his head and, relieved, she fell back into bed. She heard sounds from the kitchen and figured he must be rummaging in there for some breakfast. Lily supposed she would have to break the news to him that she didn't have anything for breakfast. As she remembered it, all the refrigerator held was a half-eaten container of yogurt and a shriveled carrot in the back of the vegetable bin.

"Good morning," Trent said cheerily as he strode into the bedroom and plopped down on the bed next to Lily. He stroked her hair affectionately. "Ready to face the day?"

Lily looked up at him and felt her heart almost stop in her chest. He was so incredibly handsome, even in the morning.

"I'll give it a try," she said, and raised herself on her elbow while she swept her hair out of her eyes.

"Too much excitement last night?" Trent grinned at her wickedly.

Lily felt her mouth go dry and her palms dampen. Last night had been more than exciting—it had been like being reborn into a brand-new wonderful world that only she and Trent shared. She felt like a completely different and totally satisfied woman.

"You're embarrassing me," she whispered to Trent, and poked him in the shoulder, then flopped down face first into her pillow to hide her blushing face. Just the memory of their night together sent tremblings through her body.

Trent placed his hand tenderly on her shoulder and felt her quaking. "Why, Lily Lansden, you're trembling." He laughed, but it was a pleased-sounding laugh.

"No I'm not," she denied, and then rolled over onto her back. "I'm usually a little shaky in the morning."

Trent leaned over and lifted her hands over her head, and then clasped them in his own. He pressed his face close to hers so that their mouths were just inches apart.

"Are you thinking about last night?" he whispered.

Lily nodded wordlessly, her eyes wide and childlike.

"So am I," Trent said. His lips hovered above hers, and she longed for her hands to be free so that she could clasp him to her and kiss his tempting mouth. "It was wonderful for me. Was it wonderful for you?"

Again Lily nodded. His black forelock fell against her cheek and tickled it. She wondered how much longer Trent could stand to wait for their kiss. He was such a tease. Finally she tore her hands out of his and drew him to her eagerly, but he held back.

"Lily, you're going to wear me out. A man has to eat, you know." He sat back up in the bed. "There's nothing in the kitchen."

Lily, disappointed, sat up and rested her head against the pillow. "I always order out for breakfast."

"Not exactly the domestic type, huh?" Trent teased.

"No, but I make up for it in other ways," she teased right back.

Trent put back his head and laughed out loud. Lily watched as the sinews in his neck stretched and then vibrated. He was so full of life, so vital and vibrant—how had she ever existed without him?

"I can't argue with that," he finally said. "Order us some breakfast, Lily, while I take a shower. Make mine a double order of everything. I'm absolutely famished." He got up and walked toward the bathroom, and when he shut the door behind him, the room seemed empty and lifeless without his presence.

Lily leaned over to the phone and dialed the coffee shop next door. They promised to bring breakfast right away.

Half an hour later she and Trent were both showered and dressed and sitting down to breakfast in the kitchen. Normally Lily just had coffee in the morning, but this morning, like Trent, she was famished. They ate companionably in silence until Trent broke it with a question.

"What are you up to today, Lily?" he asked.

She poked at the last of her eggs. "Not much."

"I was thinking . . ."

She looked up at him.

"I was thinking we should get to know each other. Now that I'm a gentleman of leisure"—he was referring to the checks that both of them had received from Albert Fountaine the previous week—"I can afford to take some time off. What do you say, Lily?" His eyes searched hers eagerly as he hoped for an encouraging reply. "Let's take the week off and play."

"Well . . ." She didn't want to appear too eager. A small part of her was still holding back from Trent and the newness of their relationship, but the larger part of her couldn't imagine anything more wonderful than spending time with him with no disturbances. "I think it's a good idea," she responded shyly.

"Great!" Trent leaned across the table and kissed her resoundingly on the lips. "I'm going to go home and pick up a few things and shave." He rubbed his stubbly chin and smiled.

A day's growth of beard added a certain rakish quality to his looks. Lily remembered how his whiskers had prickled her cheek when she had kissed him earlier that morning. Secretly, she smiled to herself. A whole week of Trent Daily. If she felt this good after just one night, imagine how she would feel after a whole week!

Trent went into the bedroom to get his jacket, while Lily picked up the remains of their breakfast and tossed it in the trash can. Just as Trent was heading back to pick up his coat on the sofa, the phone rang. Lily motioned to him to stay put while she picked it up.

"Lily, Albert. How are you?" He sounded like his usual cheery self.

"Wonderful," she replied, and then mouthed "Albert" to Trent. He smiled and sat down.

"Good. I have a job for you and Lawrence later in the week. Do you have any plans?"

'No," Lily said. The only plans she had were to enjoy Trent's company to the maximum. "What is it?"

"There's a wine buyers' convention at the Coliseum, and I'd like you two to make an appearance on Friday. It'll only be for a few hours."

"That sounds all right, but let me ask Lawrence." Lily was glad that Albert had called before Trent had left. It might have been a little difficult to explain why he wasn't there on a Sunday afternoon.

She turned to Trent and covered the mouthpiece. "Albert wants us to appear at a convention next Friday. Is that okay?"

Trent nodded in agreement and smiled at Lily.

Lily returned to the phone. "It's okay with Lawrence. When should we meet you?"

"I'll call you Thursday with the details. By the way, we're working on the commercial, and it's almost done. You two did a terrific job."

"Thanks, Albert. We enjoyed it too." Lily smiled over at Trent.

"Well, my dear, I'll let you go. Talk to you Thursday."

Lily said goodbye and hung up. She went over to Trent and began to pull him up from the couch. "Do you think we can fake it again?" she asked coquettishly.

"I don't think we have to fake being a happy couple anymore, do we, Lily?" He looked down at her, and his eyes were questioningly intense. "I haven't asked you yet, but you are happy, aren't you?"

"Deliriously," she told him again.

"Me too." He nuzzled his lips against the top of her head. "Well, if we're going to make a public appearance, I'm going to need some new clothes. What do you say tomorrow we go on a shopping spree? You can be my wardrobe consultant."

Lily smiled up at him. "I think I prefer undressing you to dressing you."

He gave her a quick hug. "Lily Lansden, I'm seeing a completely different side of you this morning."

"So am I," she sighed. "And it feels wonderful."

They held each other close, and Lily could tell that Trent was as reluctant to leave her as she was sad to see him go, even if it was only going to be for a few hours.

"I'll be back in a bit," Trent said as he broke their embrace.

They walked over to the door hand in hand, and then kissed tenderly. Lily began to feel that now-familiar stirring of longing at the base of her throat. She pulled back and playfully pushed him away.

"You'd better hightail it out of here, Trent Daily, before I kidnap you and hold you hostage in my bedroom for the rest of the week."

"Lily, you are getting downright bawdy," he said with a smile, and then caught her hand and kissed its cupped palm. "But you know I love it and . . ." He looked at her longingly as he rubbed her hand against the pricking stubble of his beard and sent little thrills of desire down her back. "I l—"

Quickly Lily took her hand and pressed it against his mouth, muffling what he was about to say. "No, not yet, not until you're really sure."

"I am sure," he insisted, his eyes glowing a rich, deep amethyst. "Aren't you?"

Lily looked at him, and with all her heart she wanted to tell him that yes, she was in love with him, too, but something held her back. "It's too soon," she answered evasively.

Trent dropped her hand and moved slightly away from her. Lily's heart clutched and thumped off beat. She didn't want to hurt him, but she could see that she was.

"It's that damned James again, isn't it, Lily?" he said.

"No, as a matter of fact." She leaned against the wall and crossed her arms over her chest. "He called last night."

"He did?"

"Yes, and revealed his true colors." Lily told Trent about the phone call. "But the funny thing was, Trent," she concluded, "I didn't really care. I stopped having feelings for James . . ." She looked down at her feet, wondering if she could trust Trent enough to tell him just what was on her mind. She decided it was time to open herself up to him. "When I met you." She looked up. Trent's face had lost its angry look and now seemed just slightly confused.

"Then what could be stopping you?" he asked ardently.

"Me, myself and I," she said. "I guess I'm still a little shell-shocked."

"Well . . ." Trent came up to her and grasped her firmly by the shoulders. "We have a whole week ahead of us, Lily, and in that week I'm going to try to convince you that I am absolutely, irrevocably and utterly in love with you."

"And what about me?" Lily asked. "Do I have to do the same?"

"That's your decision," Trent answered firmly. "But I don't see how you'll be able to resist," he said with a straight face.

"Oh, you." Lily swatted him playfully. "Get out of here before we start to fight again."

Trent grabbed her hand and his face was newly serious. "No more fights, Lily. Deal?" His gaze was intense.

"Deal," she answered, and kissed him lightly. "Hurry back, Trent. I'll miss you," she said, and meant it. Already he was beginning to seem as necessary to her as air.

"Me too," he said, and opened the door. "Is there anything I can bring you on my way back?"

"Just bring yourself," Lily replied. "You're more than enough."

7

Monday, Tuesday, Wednesday—the days with Trent all blurred together in Lily's mind, each one of them perfect. They visited museums and art galleries, sipped espresso in Greenwich Village, where Trent lived, and shopped on Madison Avenue near Lily's penthouse. They spent the evenings at the theater or taking in a film. One night they even stayed up until daybreak, dancing at a rock club and breakfasting at a seedy diner on Tenth Avenue, as truck drivers ambled in and out, eyeing them curiously.

For Lily, being with Trent was like being with no one else she had ever known. He could be wildly impulsive, buying her little trinkets because they had caught her eye, or suggesting that they hop on the Staten Island ferry just for the fun of it and then insisting that they ride back and forth five times simply because the sea spray made Lily's face glow in such a charming fashion. He could be deadly serious when they got into a discussion about literature, opening up ways of thinking about things that Lily had never even considered before. In public he was the consummate gentleman, opening doors, pulling out chairs, removing wraps, hailing taxis— all as if he were to the manor born. In private, as her lover, he was fiercely demanding and then tenderly reciprocating. Quite simply, he took Lily's breath away.

Finally, late on Thursday afternoon, when it seemed as if they'd exhausted everything the city had to offer and as the sun was beginning to set in an orange sky, Trent brought Lily downtown to his apartment in Greenwich

Village. It was a tiny box of a place, with the kitchen in the living room and the bathtub in the kitchen, and no closets. Trent seemed to use the floor to hang up his clothes. On a stack of orange crates in one corner sat an old battered manual typewriter. Lily thought of her fancy electric and her typist and shuddered.

"How can you write here?" she asked him, genuinely perplexed.

Trent merely walked over to the typewriter, pulled out an old wooden chair that was missing half of its struts and teetered wildly, sat down and began to pound away.

"It's easy," he yelled over the racket of the typewriter. "Got nothing to distract me."

He was right. The only window in the apartment faced an air shaft, and all there was to be seen were rows and rows of dirty bricks.

Trent shuffled around in some stacks of papers next to the crates. "Would you like to see what I've been working on?" he asked, handing her a sheaf of typewritten pages.

Lily accepted the papers gingerly. She had been reluctant to see what it was that Trent wrote for fear that she'd either not like it, or like it so much that she'd be intimidated by his talent.

"It may be a little hard to read. I do a lot of rewriting," he apologized as Lily scrutinized the pages. Some of them were so filled with pencil scrawlings and minuscule inserts in the margins that they were almost illegible.

"I'll try," she sighed, and sat down on Trent's unmade sofa bed.

"I'll make us some coffee while you're at it," Trent said, and then left her alone to read.

Fifteen minutes later Lily was finished with what Trent had given her, and her only wish was that he had given her more. The characters were so real that Lily felt as if she almost knew them, and the style was clean and fresh and utterly captivating. She put the pages down with a sigh. Clearly Trent was a writer to the bone.

He came up to her with a cracked mug of coffee. "Do you like it?"

Lily sipped at the hot coffee slowly, wanting to choose her words carefully so they'd convey exactly what she thought. "It's one of the best things I've ever read."

Trent sat beside her in silence, but the glow on his face showed his pleasure at her approval.

"Do you have more?" she asked.

"This is part of a novel that I've just finished. I didn't think it was good enough to include."

If what she had read was what Trent had rejected as not being good enough, Lily knew that what he had kept had to be extraordinary. "Has anyone seen this?" she asked tentatively. Perhaps she could help him place it with an agent.

He took the pages out of her hands and riffled them nervously, then looked at her with the strangest expression on his face, almost as if he were trying to gather courage. "I showed it to Bev," he said softly and quickly.

Lily shot off the bed. "You showed it to Bev!" Now it all seemed so clear. "That's why you took this job as my husband. So you could find yourself an agent!"

"Of course the money didn't enter into it at all," Trent said sarcastically.

"That has nothing to do with it. You're just using me, and you're using Bev. What about that little speech you gave me in Connecticut? Where's your artistic integrity now? You forced your book on Bev, and then you lied to me. . . ." She slumped back on the bed, feeling as if her heart would break. Trent was turning out to be just like James—he only wanted to use her.

She could feel hot, painful tears welling up in her eyes. She gritted her teeth and balled her hands into fists, willing herself not to cry. The last thing in the world she wanted was to let Trent see how much she hurt. But she had to turn her face away from him when her willpower proved unable to control the tears that spilled over and coursed down her cheeks. Now she was hoping that she'd be able to stop the sobs she felt beginning to heave in her chest. She had thought that she'd finally found someone to love, but now she knew that it had all been just a game for Trent. Until Bev agreed to be his agent he would pretend to be in love with Lily, and then, when he'd gotten what he wanted, he'd drop her. How could life be so unfair?

She thought she was going to suffocate if she held her breath any longer as she tried to stop sobbing, and then Trent touched her shoulder softly and murmured her name. The mere touch of his hand finally broke her pride. She began to weep openly in front of him, and she despised herself for being so weak willed.

"Lily, oh, Lily," Trent whispered, and took her in his arms. "You suspect all the wrong things." He stroked her hair lovingly.

Just being in his arms seemed to soothe her sobbing away. There had to be an explanation. "What am I supposed to think?"

"Lily, Bev asked to see my book," Trent said.

"She did?" Lily's eyes were wide with disbelief. "Why didn't she tell me? Why didn't you tell me?" Now that the tears had passed, Lily was beginning to feel angry. Why hadn't Bev told her? Or had she begun to that day in Connecticut, and then backed off when Lily's reaction to her suggestion that Trent might be a good writer was so negative? But Trent could have told her, and he had chosen not to.

Trent crumpled the pages in his hands and then threw them down on the floor. "Because I knew you'd react like this. I thought we'd gotten to the point where you trusted me and could be rational about my being a writer, too, but I can see I was wrong."

"Trust you! How can I trust you when you don't tell me the truth?" Lily snapped back and pulled herself out of his embrace. There *was* no explanation.

"I didn't lie to you, Lily. I just didn't want to tell you until I heard from Bev what she thought about it. I spoke with her today, so I decided to talk to you." Trent said the words as if he were being perfectly reasonable about the matter.

"When did you talk to Bev?" Lily asked. They had been together every second of the day. She didn't remember his talking to Bev.

"You were in the shower this morning when the phone rang, remember? Since I was there, I talked to her then."

"Oh," Lily said.

Trent shook his head impatiently. "Well, you don't have to worry—she's not going to be my agent. . . ."

Lily raised her eyebrows. Maybe she was a fool making such a fuss when Bev hadn't even liked his work.

"She's sending it to Martin Gibson," he finished.

"Martin Gibson!" Lily exclaimed. Gibson was the most famous literary agent in the country, and he handled only the very best writers. If a writer was handled by Gibson, it meant he was the *crème de la crème* of the literary establishment. Is that what Trent would be? And if it was, where did that leave her?

Lily turned cool. "That's nice," was all she finally said.

Trent looked at her, obviously perplexed. "I don't understand you, Lily. First you're upset to the point of tears, then you're angry, and now you act as if you don't care. Why don't you tell me how you really feel?"

"Why? Is it important to you?" Lily didn't see how it could be.

"Yes, it's damned important to me. I thought you'd be pleased that I might have a chance at success."

Lily decided to continue to play cool. She didn't want Trent to know that the thought of his success disturbed her in a way she couldn't yet define. "I think it's wonderful." She smiled and hoped Trent wouldn't see the insincerity that lay beneath it.

Trent looked at her, and it seemed as if he saw right

through her with his clear gaze. "You're threatened by this, aren't you? Damn it, Lily, why are you so insecure about your own abilities as a writer?"

"I'm not," she protested, but she knew that he had found the heart of the problem. Hadn't she tried to do the kind of writing that Trent seemed to do so effortlessly, and hadn't she failed?

Something must have told Trent not to pursue the matter any further, because he surprised Lily with what he finally said after he'd scrutinized her closely for a few moments. "I know you're holding back, Lily," he said, and then placed his fingers across her mouth when she tried to deny his statement. "No, don't say anything. Whatever it is you feel, it's something you're going to have to deal with yourself. You're the only one who can exorcise those little demons inside you that tell you you're less than the wonderful writer that everyone, including me, knows you are. If I have to, I'll wait."

He removed his hand from her mouth and then gazed into her eyes forthrightly. "I love you, Lily, and I'll wait."

As she looked at Trent and saw the love shining in his eyes, she realized that, more than anything else in the world, she wanted to banish those demons from her life. She knew that if she didn't, she'd lose him, and it wouldn't be anyone's fault but her own. Because Trent was right. Whatever barrier there was between them was of her creation. It wasn't her success, or his possible success, or James, or anything that had happened in the past—it was something else, some insecurity of her own that she would have to conquer.

She clasped Trent's hand in her own and tenderly touched his cheek. "I won't make you wait long. I promise."

The tenderness she had felt for him turned into pure fire when he pressed his lips against hers. Inflamed, she molded her body to him and rubbed her tender breasts against his hard chest, and the fire coursed through her veins and ignited the center of her desire. It was always that way when Trent touched her now. Always the hot, greedy response to his hands and mouth, always the hungry yearning gnawing at her insides, as if she couldn't get enough of him.

Lily marveled at the man Trent was as he continued to caress her body. He could be tender, and yet it didn't make him seem any less manly; he could be fiercely demanding as a lover, and yet it didn't make him seem selfish; he could take complete control of her senses with his strong physicality, and yet he was never brutal. He took as much as he gave, and he always knew when to do each. He was the most enormously perceptive man she had ever known. Lily knew that when he made love to her, he did it with his heart and soul, not merely his body.

Trent pressed her down onto the bed, his hands traveling the length of her thighs with a feverishness that matched her own, pushing up her skirt to find the soft flesh at the tops of her silk stockings. Their mouths locked in a kiss as their tongues lapped and entwined, darted and drew back in a teasing, exciting dance. Their hands smoothed and then inflamed each other's flesh, touching each other hard and then softly, fingers kneading with a whisper touch, and then pressing with deep, rhythmic strokes until they could stand to be apart no longer.

Trent began to remove Lily's clothing a piece at a time. As each spot of her flesh was exposed, he surveyed it as if he had just discovered some marvelous new treasure, and then he kissed and anointed it with his lips, as if preparing her for a sacred ritual. Lily felt cherished, worshiped, as Trent finally freed her of the last vestiges of clothing and she lay next to him on the bed, completely naked, as he feasted his eyes on her wanton loveliness.

Trent stood beside the bed and undressed before her, and as his clothing fell to the floor, Lily thrilled to the sight of each part of his lithe and muscular body. His arms were strong and muscular, his chest smooth and taut and hard like a Greek warrior's, his legs well developed, with bulging masculine calves. Finally he removed the last piece of clothing and Lily could see just how much he wanted her. She closed her eyes and reveled in the sensation of being completely and utterly desired.

He lay next to her, his cool flesh heating up next to hers. She threw her arms around his neck and pulled him against her, almost wishing that she could crawl into his skin, her need for him was so overwhelming. There was an urgency between them that, even in their previous passions, had never been expressed as forcefully.

He rolled her over onto her back and nudged between her thighs with his knees. She opened her legs to him—there was nothing she would deny him. He entered her with a deep, forceful stroke, and at last her emptiness was filled. She felt as if he had entered her very soul as she arched her body fiercely against his, seeking even more of him, wanting everything he had to give. They rocked together on the bed until it was clear that neither of them could hold back any longer.

Lily opened her eyes and saw Trent's above her, glowing in the dark twilight. They burned like wildfire, like unborn amethysts buried deep within the earth, still molten and fire-charged.

"Lily, oh, Lily." His eyes blazed as he repeated her name over and over, and then she saw the pupils of his eyes widen and felt her own opening and taking his in like sparking meteors flying through the star-struck skies, as together they seemed to shoot through the heavens, earthbound no longer.

Later, as they lay entwined in perfect contentment, Lily's mind floated lazily. Satisfied and fulfilled, she could feel it begin to clear. Trent was right—it was time to banish her demons. He knew about her failure with James, but of her other failure—the one that hurt most—he knew nothing. Perhaps it was time to tell him.

She extricated her limbs from his, turned on her side and caressed him with her free hand. His skin was taut and supple beneath her fingers as she trailed them down his chest and then over to his sides, where she tickled him lightly. He squirmed deliciously, and when he laughed his voice was throaty and rough with spent passion. She prayed that there would never be a day when he wouldn't relish her touch, nor she his.

"Trent, there's something I want you to know." She brushed his tousled hair out of his eyes so she could see his reaction to what she had to say.

"Yes?" He pressed her hand against his lips and nuzzled her sensitive palm, then began to nibble at her wrist and the soft underside of her forearm. If she didn't stop him, Lily knew, he'd continue until he was kissing parts even more sensitive than those he already had, and she'd never get to tell him what was weighing on her mind.

"Stop that," she chided. "I have important things to say."

"All right." Trent sat up and placed his hands behind his ears, pressing them forward. "I'm all ears."

Lily looked at him, and then burst out laughing. "How can I be serious when you look like Dumbo the elephant?"

He removed his hands from his ears and placed them on either side of her face as he gazed intently into her eyes. "It's just that you looked so serious. . . ." He pursed his lips and mimicked a frown. "And I don't feel serious. I feel . . . well, I feel more wonderful than I ever thought was possible." He caressed the tender crescent behind her ear with a touch that was as feathery and light as a moth's wing.

She lowered her eyes and said softly, "I do too, Trent. It is wonderful to be with you. But there's something I want you to know."

"Go ahead, Lily." He leaned back on the bed. "Please tell me."

"You wondered before why I was so sensitive about my talents as a writer. . . ."

"Completely unjustified," he said firmly.

He was so sure of her. He had such faith. Why didn't she have it for herself?

"Once I wrote a serious novel," she blurted out. "It was awful. Bev refused to even say anything about it after I showed it to her, except that she thought I should stick to writing mysteries. I failed, don't you see?"

Trent laughed. "Lily, is that your secret, that you failed once at writing something?"

"Yes," she said, confused. Why was he laughing? It hadn't been funny to her, it had been shattering.

"Oh, Lily. How can I explain to you . . . ?" He sat up in bed and then swung his legs over the side. "Wait. I'll show you."

He turned on a light, then went over to the piles of paper around his makeshift desk and began to shuffle through them impatiently.

"Ah, here they are." He came back to the bed carrying a manila folder stuffed with papers. He placed it on the bed next to her. "Open it up."

Lily opened the folder and found the first piece of paper. It was a letter. She looked up at Trent questioningly.

"Rejection letters," he said. "I stopped counting after the twentieth, but I saved every one of them."

Quickly, Lily scanned several of them. Some of the comments were only mildly insulting; others were so derogatory they must have been devastating. One editor even insisted that his seven-year-old child could write better than Trent could—with one arm tied behind her back. Lily closed the folder quickly. She couldn't stand to read any more. How had he managed to go on writing?

Trent sat down beside her. "See, Lily, you're not the only one who's been told their writing stinks. Being rejected is something that all writers go through. And look at you." Lily looked down and saw that she was naked. Self-consciously, she wrapped the top sheet around her.

"You've only been rejected once. Bev's loved everything else, right?"

Lily nodded in agreement. She felt like a fool in light of what Trent was telling her now.

Playfully, he chucked her under the chin. "See, Lily, you were perfect and you didn't even know it."

She smiled shyly. How was it that Trent could take the things she feared the most and miraculously turn them into things that needn't be feared at all? She gazed into his eyes. They were like brimming goblets of sweet purple wine, and she drank of them until she felt totally intoxicated. Then she finally said what she had felt in her heart for such a long time but had been afraid to admit.

"I love you, Trent," she murmured, and wound her hands through the coal black strands of his hair as she pulled him close.

"I love you, too, Lily," he said, caressing her and showing her just how true his words were.

The next morning they hopped into a cab and rode up to Lily's penthouse. They had to breakfast, shower and dress before Albert Fountaine's limousine arrived at ten to take them to the wine buyers' convention.

Shortly before ten, they were ready, Trent in an immaculate and perfectly tailored gray pinstripe suit, and Lily in a gray pleated dress that was simple and elegant when worn with her black pearls and black suede pumps.

"Is my tie straight?" Trent asked Lily as he fiddled with the knot. "I'm not used to wearing these damned things."

Lily ran to his side and slapped his fussing hands away. "It's perfectly fine, and you look wonderful."

He let his eyes graze her figure as she stood before him. "And so do you. When's that limousine due?" He gave her a good-natured leer. "Maybe there's time . . ."

The buzzer rang as if right on cue.

"I've heard of quickies, Trent, but I think we'd be setting a new record."

He lunged for the phone. "Maybe we should call up the *Guinness Book of World Records* and . . ."

Lily stopped him before he went any further. She loved the bawdy bantering they'd begun to indulge in together. It made every second that she was with him seem alive with possibilities, but right now Albert was waiting for them downstairs. "Come on." She tapped him on the shoulder. "It can wait until later." She headed out the apartment door, Trent hot on her heels.

"I don't think it can, Lily." Trent glanced over at her as they waited in the hall for the car to arrive. "That look" was beginning to develop in his eyes. "You know, your elevator is very cozy. What do you say . . . ?"

The elevator stopped at their floor, the doors opened and Trent gave her a quick push through them. She stumbled into the car—straight into the arms of Albert Fountaine.

"Lily!" he exclaimed as he gathered her up and kissed her. "Such a friendly girl," he murmured to Trent over Lily's shoulder.

"Albert!" Lily managed to choke out his name.

"I was just coming up to prod you along in case you might be running late." He smiled happily. "But I can see that both of you are raring to go."

Lily smiled at him weakly.

"Do you always wake up this perky?" Albert asked.

Lily looked at Trent, and her look was begging him to get them out of this.

"No." Trent cleared his throat. "Lily and I were about to set a new record—"

Lily stabbed her elbow into his side. He wasn't going to tell Albert what they had been talking about, was he?

Trent grabbed her elbow, and then slid her arm through his. "We were about to set a new record for being on time," he finished lamely, and then he looked at Lily and they both burst into peals of laughter.

"Some kind of in-joke here that I'm missing?" Albert questioned them, feigning gravity.

They kept laughing together until the elevator doors opened onto the lobby.

"You two seem different today," Albert said as they walked to the door. "No more battling Lansdens?"

"We've declared a truce," Trent said as they passed through to the street.

"Well, that's fine," Albert said as he slid into the car and motioned to them to follow him into the back seat. "Just don't get sappy about it. I liked that . . ." He paused to find the right word. ". . . edge you used to have."

Lily sat between the two men. "Don't worry, Albert. Lawrence still has his cranky moods."

"And Lily still has her bad temper," Trent retorted as he began to glower at her.

Albert beamed. "That's wonderful. Now you're the Lily and Lawrence I love."

Lily and Trent smiled at each other happily.

"Now, about this convention . . ." Albert got down to business.

"What do you want us to do?" Lily asked.

"Basically, it's a piece of cake. We have a big corner of one of the convention floors all set up for the Fountaine Winery. All you and Lawrence have to do is smile, drink a lot of champagne and get everyone else to drink a lot of champagne. Then, when we have the buyers at our mercy"—Albert grinned and rubbed his hands together —"my salesmen move in and take orders."

"That sounds easy," said Trent.

"It is. Oh, and by the way, the commercial's all done. We didn't even need any dubbing; it was perfect. We'll be showing it today on television monitors."

"Great," Lily and Trent said in unison.

"I can't wait to see it," Lily continued.

"It's quite good." Albert glowed proudly. "It'll start running just as soon as I can arrange for the airtime. In a month or so, I imagine."

Lily looked over to Trent to see what his reaction was. For some reason he looked uneasy. What could be bothering him about the commercial? Was he afraid he might look bad, or seem silly? She gave him a questioning look, but he ignored it.

The limousine turned into Columbus Circle, and then stopped in front of the Coliseum. While they rode the escalator up to the second floor, Lily examined Trent's face for the expression she had seen before, but it was gone. Now he looked perfectly normal. She decided that it must have been another instance of her overactive imagination at work.

The area that Albert had rented for the Fountaine Winery was large and well placed, just to one side of the escalator. A fountain that had been set up in the middle of the display and was already spurting champagne was a real eye-catcher, and low sofas and miniature palm trees scattered about turned the area into a pleasant oasis. Lily imagined that quite a few of the buyers wouldn't be able to resist the lure of a refreshing drink and a place to sit down and rest their feet. Two television monitors had been placed on either end of the exhibition area, and another one was hanging from the ceiling. Obviously Albert had put a lot of effort into the exhibition.

"What do you think?" he asked her cheerfully, knowing that she could only approve.

"It's great. Where do you want Lawrence and me to stand?"

"I think right by the fountain. You can fill glasses and pass them out. I'll stay right with you to make introductions."

A young man edged up to them and looked at Albert eagerly. "And here's someone who obviously wants an introduction right now." He gestured to the young man. "Lily and Lawrence Lansden, this is Bob Goldschmidt. He's our salesman on the West Coast."

Bob wasted no time. He clasped Lily's hand anxiously and kept holding on to it, while Trent, who had also extended his hand, was left with it hanging in midair.

"I've been waiting for this day for months, Mrs.

Lansden. I'm one of your biggest fans," Bob said ardently.

Lily shook his hand and then gently extricated hers from his avid grip. "Isn't that nice?" she said. "This is my husband, Lawrence." She reintroduced Trent, who was standing a trifle uneasily at her side.

Bob gave Trent's hand a quick shake and then dropped it like a dead fish. He returned to Lily.

"I love your books. I loved that part in *Death's Deceiver* when you had the murderer trip over the cat's tail and drop the key that gave him away to the police. It was so right, so natural—"

Lily interrupted him before he got carried away with his adjectives. "Thank you." She smiled at him winningly.

"And then, in *The Lady Is Dead,* when you had that society lady fall into a dish of dog food and choke to death. Wow!" At this point he grabbed his hair and pulled it for emphasis. "It was so neat!"

"Are you an animal lover?" Trent asked him dryly. Lily could tell already that Trent did not like being ignored.

Bob looked over at Trent as if he were a member of the vice squad who had accidentally stumbled into an orgy. Obviously he had put a damper on the young man's enthusiasm. "No," Bob sniffed. "I just like mysteries."

"Well, I'm glad to hear that." Lily was overwhelmingly cheery back to him to compensate for Trent's lack of politeness.

Albert must have sensed that something was slowly going awry, because he latched on to Bob's arm and pulled him aside on the pretext of talking to him about some orders that had come into the office the previous week.

Lily had turned to Trent and opened her mouth to ask him what the matter was, when she caught a glimpse of something that left her with her mouth hanging open. Coming up the escalator was a solid line of men in business suits, and each and every one of them, as he stepped off, was heading straight toward the Fountaine exhibition, as if the champagne fountain held some kind of elixir of youth and they were in dread danger of keeling over from old age.

"Well," Trent said to her, "to paraphrase Bette Davis, Lily, 'Fasten your seat belts; it's going to be a rocky ride!'" He planted a smile on his face, stuck out his hand and nudged Lily to do the same.

By four o'clock Lily's smile was about to crack her face. Her hand was red and sore from shaking the hands of so many well-wishers, and she had drunk so much champagne that she was in danger of floating away. At least at autographing parties only her writing hand got sore, but here even her back hurt from being pounded by some of the more gregarious wine merchants. Trent stood beside her, looking as if he were about to explode.

If the worst of it had been that he had been ignored, that would have been bad enough, but some of the buyers, in their nervousness at meeting Lily Lansden in the flesh, had treated Trent as if he were some kind of stuffed mascot or, even worse, a combination butler-secretary. Too many times for Lily to count, Trent had had to explain that, no, he didn't do her typing for her, and no, he didn't want to write at all, one writer was more than enough in a marriage, and yes, sometimes he helped Lily with her plots, and yes, he knew all too well what a genius his wife was.

Lily herself had her own problems. It seemed as if everyone she met had a friend, or a relative, or a friend of a relative who wrote mystery novels and was desperately in need of a publisher, or at least someone to read their masterpiece. She had to tell them all gently that she wished she could help, but she was much too busy writing her own new mystery. Then she refluffed their flattened spirits with a few inside tips on what the new book was about.

Now the crowd was beginning to thin out, and Lily finally had a chance to breathe. Plastic cups littered the carpet around the fountain, and several buyers were conked out on the sofas—too much champagne. Lily wished she could do the same. At lunchtime Albert had brought sandwiches for her and Trent, but she had had just enough time to wolf half of hers down in the ladies' room and then she had had to reenter the fray. She was starving, slightly drunk, and exhausted beyond belief. Wearily she looked over at Trent and gave him a halfhearted smile. He didn't return it.

"I thought Albert said it was going to be a couple of hours," he grumbled. "We've been here six already."

"I don't think he thought we were going to be such a hit. Do you know how many orders he's taken? He showed me about an hour ago. It's amazing. And it's all because of *us.*" She emphasized the last word.

"Because of you, Lily. I'm just your husband, remember?"

"Oh, Tr—" Damn it, Lily was having a devilishly hard time remembering that in public she had to call him Lawrence. "It's the commercial, Lawrence." She smiled as an inebriated buyer lumbered by. "And you're in the commercial, remember?"

"Just barely. The camera's always on you." Lily was surprised at his bad temper, although she couldn't really blame him. Somehow, most of the shots of Trent had been inexplicably lost in the cutting room. Mostly you just saw his hand—pouring Fountaine champagne.

"Well . . ." Lily was at a loss for words, and then it became irrelevant. A bulky-looking gentleman had plopped himself in front of them and was smiling from ear to ear.

"Lily Lansden," he gushed.

"Hello, it's nice to meet you." By now the greeting came effortlessly to her lips, and for that Lily was glad. If she really said what was on her mind . . . well, it wouldn't be very polite, and it certainly wouldn't sell champagne.

"And this must be Lawrence." He reached over and pumped Trent's hand.

"Hello," Trent said, barely suppressing a grimace as the man squeezed his hand in a death grip.

The man turned back to Lily. "Is this the guy you based Dash Chadbourne on?" He looked at Trent as if he could hardly believe it was possible.

"Yes," Lily said brightly. "Can't you tell? They're both so suave and debonair."

"Hmm." The man gave Trent the once-over, and it was obvious that he didn't agree with the comparison.

Lily was about to jolly him out of his disbelief when Trent interrupted. "Lily love, I'll be back in a minute." And then he disappeared. It was the fastest vanishing act Lily had ever seen. She continued to make pleasant conversation with the man until, satisfied that he had had enough contact with her to brag about to his friends, he left.

Lily was looking around, trying to discover where Trent had disappeared to, when Albert appeared at her elbow. "I just saw Lawrence go downstairs," he said nonchalantly. "I think you two have had enough for one day."

"I think so too, Albert."

"You've been great. I can't tell you how much I appreciate your help." He patted her fondly on the shoulder.

"Did Lawrence say where he was going?" Lily asked anxiously.

"Something about a cup of coffee," Albert replied. "There's a coffee shop around the corner; maybe that's where he went."

He looked at Lily quizzically. "It must be tough for him," he said.

"He's used to it by now," Lily lied. She didn't want Albert to know just how fed up with the whole business Trent was. "I'm going to go down and find him."

"Good. Keep in touch," Albert said.

Lily didn't wait for the escalator to carry her to the main floor; she ran down the moving steps, almost falling in her haste to find Trent. It had been rude of him just to disappear like that, but she couldn't blame him. They had had a long, hard day.

She ran out to the street, and only when she was hit with a blast of freezing air did she realize that she'd left her fur upstairs. She turned to run back in, but she was so impatient to find Trent that she changed her mind and headed down the street. Albert had said the coffee shop was nearby. She was sure she'd find Trent before she had much of a chance to freeze.

Halfway down the block she found the coffee shop and darted through the door. She looked around, but Trent was nowhere to be seen. Well, she rationalized, there must be another coffee shop further down the block; he was probably there.

Lily had checked out three more coffee shops and her teeth were chattering with cold before she finally found Trent in a little diner five blocks away from the Coliseum. He was sitting all alone in a booth, with three cups of coffee lined up in front of him. She slid in opposite him without saying a word and grabbed one of the cups of coffee.

"Good idea," she said enthusiastically. "Time to sober up."

Trent didn't seem startled by her sudden appearance; he merely pushed over the sugar bowl and the creamer and then returned to finishing up his first cup. They drank in silence until he was halfway through his second, and then Lily couldn't stand the tension between them anymore.

"That was a mighty quick vanishing act you pulled back there," she said. How could she tell him that she didn't blame him for it, and that she understood how ghastly the whole experience must have been for him?

Trent merely continued to sip his coffee, his face inscrutable.

"Aren't you going to talk to me?" she asked him angrily. It had been a bad day, certainly, but it hadn't been her fault!

Trent turned to her then and spoke slowly, weighing each word in his mind before it escaped his mouth. "That's not what you hired me for," he said flatly.

"What are you saying?" Lily was aghast. Was he angry at her for the rudeness of the buyers at the convention? That wasn't fair.

"I'm saying that I did my job. I was Lily Lansden's husband, and just between you and me, Lily . . ." He glowered at her. "The job stinks."

"But, Trent," she spluttered, almost choking on her coffee. "That has nothing to do with us. That's Lawrence, not Trent."

"You know"—he leaned back in the booth and crossed his arms over his chest—"before we did this damned thing today, I was actually wondering what it might be like to be your husband. . . ."

Lily's eyes opened wide. Had Trent been thinking that he wanted to marry her? The thought had occurred to her, too, and up until this moment it had seemed like a completely wonderful idea.

"Now I know what it's like. Lily Lansden's husband has about as much status as a pet dog." He slammed his coffee cup down into its saucer and began to rise from the booth. Lily grabbed his hand and forced him back down.

"Trent . . ." She tried to calm herself and think logically and rationally. "I know it must have been awful for you. I'm so sorry. But that was just today. What about the rest of the week we've spent together?"

"I've been thinking about that," he said with a thoughtful look on his face.

She was getting through to him at last. If he thought

about the rest of the week, there was no way he could be angry. The time they'd spent together had been glorious.

"Where did we spend all our time together?" he asked.

Lily was baffled. "We visited museums and saw some films and went to the theater. Is that what you mean?"

"No, Lily. That's not what I mean. Where did we spend our nights?"

"At my penthouse."

"Exactly."

"But we spent last night at your apartment, Trent." Lily remembered the cramped little box Trent called home. Why would they want to spend any more of their time there? Her penthouse was so much more pleasant.

Trent smiled at her, but it was a smile without any warmth. "And what about tonight?" he shot back. "Will we spend tonight at my place?"

"What does it matter?" Lily almost screamed across at him. "I'll move into your damn apartment if that's what you want."

Trent shook his head. "Lily, you'd be no happier in that apartment than the Queen of Sheba would be in Brooklyn Heights. It just won't work," he said finally.

"But we've shared so much," Lily protested, her eyes beginning to fill with tears. Was Trent telling her that it was all over?

"*We* haven't shared anything, Lily. *You've* shared with me," Trent said adamantly. "That kind of arrangement might have been fine with James what's his name, but it's not fine with me. I don't like being Lily Lansden's consort. I don't want to use you. I have my pride, and—"

"That's just it!" Lily exclaimed angrily. "It's your damn pride. You still can't bear my success, can you, Trent?"

"That's not it at all. Maybe I'm being old-fashioned about this, or maybe I'm being immature and selfish." His eyes met hers, and they were troubled. "Maybe I *am* a little envious of your success. I know that what I'm saying doesn't reflect well on me." He banged his hand on the table. "But damn it, Lily, a man likes to feel as if he's at least equal in accomplishments to the woman he's in love with. A man needs his pride. He's nothing without it."

"Are you saying that if you were successful as a writer, everything would be fine?" Now they were getting to the crux of the matter.

"I don't know how fine things would be, but at least I wouldn't feel like Lily Lansden's pampered pet."

"But Bev, and Martin Gibson . . ." she reminded him.

"Who's to say that I won't be adding Martin Gibson's letter to my rejection file?" he shot back.

"I still don't see why it matters so much to you! Why do you have to measure your worth in success? Isn't it enough that *you* know you're a writer?" Lily pleaded.

Trent looked at her for a long time before he answered. "All I have to say to you, Lily, is this: Put the shoe on the other foot and see how it feels. You're a writer; it shouldn't be hard to imagine. Then you'll have your answer."

Trent threw five dollars down onto the table. "The coffee's on me," he barked, and then strode away.

Lily had to force herself not to run after him. Was he leaving her for good, or would he change his mind when he cooled down? Oh, what did it matter? Even when he had cooled down, they would still have the same problem. She was successful and he wasn't, and for some dumb reason that had to do with his idiotic male pride, it made all the difference in the world to him.

Lily leaned her forehead on her hand and stared down at the empty coffee cups. She was sobered up now. In fact, she'd never been so sober in her entire life. She loved Trent with all her heart, and she had thought—no, she had been convinced—that he loved her. How did that old cliché go? Love conquers all? Apparently whoever had coined it had never known Trent Daily.

8

After Trent left, Lily hailed a cab outside the diner and headed over to the Coliseum to pick up her fur. Albert was still there, nudging some of the buyers who were still conked out on the couches and reminding them gently that it was time to go home. He fetched her coat from behind one of the partitions. Lily hoped that Albert wouldn't say anything about Trent's absence, and he didn't. He merely draped the fur over her shoulders and patted her back sympathetically. He must have known that whatever the problem was, Lily didn't want to talk about it.

When she got home she threw herself down on her bed and let her weary body sink into the thick mattress. She was tired to the bone. She took her phone off the hook and fell into an uneasy sleep, and she didn't wake up until the next morning. She stumbled into the bathroom to splash some cold water on her face, but when she grabbed for a towel on the rack, she found instead she was drying her face with Trent's robe. She could smell the scent of him still on it. She buried her face in it and began to cry. How was it possible to miss one person so desperately? When James had left her she had been lonely, but not with the kind of gnawing emptiness that ached within her now.

She went to the living room, looked out the window and noticed that it was snowing. How was it that everything was conspiring that morning to remind her of Trent? She remembered how the snow had clung to his thick black lashes so that they looked as if they had been dipped in sugar, and how his eyes were sometimes like plump purple grapes. And then she remembered what it was like to have his hands caress her flesh, and the way his voice sounded when he cried her name in ecstasy. She put her hands up to her head and squeezed as if she could crush the memories of him out of her mind.

When she wandered back into the bedroom she found even more traces of Trent. A sock peeked out from beneath the bedspread, and his hairbrush was balanced on the edge of her bureau. She picked it up and found strands of his hair caught in the bristles. Rubbing a black strand between her fingers, she remembered how she loved to run her hands through his hair, how fine and silken to the touch it was, and how an ebony shock of it fell over his right eye and gave him a rakish look that always tore at her heart no matter where they were. She remembered being in a restaurant with him and looking into his eyes, remembered seeing the desire spark in their violet depths and feeling the same desire flash like wildfire through her own veins.

Lily slammed the brush down. This was ridiculous! Why was she mooning over Trent Daily? He was obstinate and proud and envious and resentful. He'd taken the money and agreed to play her husband, and now, when the job was getting too tough for him, he was complaining that it was undignified, or some such nonsense. Well, Lily thought to herself, it hadn't been undignified to accept Albert's check, had it? And what he'd said about being her husband . . . ! Now that she was fully awake, Lily was remembering everything that he'd said the day before and her ire was beginning to rise. Maybe she should just pick up the phone, call Bev and sue him for breach of contract. That would show him!

Lily went over to the table beside her bed and noticed that the phone was still off the hook. What if Trent had been trying to call her last night? But then she quickly reasoned that even if he had, it certainly wouldn't have been a call she would have wanted to receive. She wanted nothing more to do with him. Just one call to Bev and she'd show Trent Daily that he couldn't say the kinds of things he had said yesterday and get away with it. . . . But wait! She stopped punching Bev's number and put the receiver back down. Bev would probably just laugh at her. Tell her that she was being oversensitive, or, even worse, she'd probably side with Trent. Bev always seemed to take Trent's side of things. And if she did try to sue Trent, then Albert would find out that they weren't married. No, if she stirred anything up, she'd suffer just as much as Trent would. Maybe even more. The whole world would know that Lily Lansden had had to hire a husband.

"Oh, damn." Lily flopped face down on her bed and began to pound the pillow. "That man, that man . . . I'd like to strangle him!"

She grabbed the pillow and began to squeeze it ferociously. She pummeled it with all her strength; then she threw it against the wall and watched as the ticking burst and feathers floated like dry snowflakes onto the bedroom carpet.

"Aaargh!" she screamed, and flopped back onto the bed. She was so good at figuring things out in her books; why was she such a complete nincompoop when it came to figuring out her own life?

If she were a character in one of her novels, she'd already have dreamed up some devious way to trip up Trent Daily. But she wasn't a character in a novel; she was just a woman, a woman very much in love with a man, and she supposed that was why all her good sense flew right out the window whenever she even thought of Trent. There was no use in attempting to scheme against him. She'd probably only bungle it if she tried.

But there was no use in mooning about him either. Lily ran to the hall closet, grabbed a cardboard box and came back into the bedroom. At least she could put all of his things away. Advice-to-the-lovelorn columnists were always saying that when you broke up with someone, you should destroy the photographs, put the trinkets and mementos away, and just start afresh. Lily grabbed for the first thing she saw—a sock. She held it up in front of her face. Was it a trinket or a memento? She tossed it into the box, along with his robe and his brush and a pair of boxer shorts that had been tossed on a chair by the bed. She remembered removing them a few nights ago and then it hit her—she'd never see Trent's lithe body next to hers again. She was just about to dissolve into tears when the phone rang.

"Hello, Lily." It was Trent.

"Hello," she said tentatively. Was he going to apologize? Was he going to admit that he had missed her as much as she missed him?

"Ahem," he cleared his throat nervously. He *is* going to apologize, Lily thought triumphantly. Humility always made Trent Daily nervous. It was a feeling he so rarely had.

"I believe I left a few things at your apartment," he finally said.

"I was just packing them up. I'll send them over by messenger." He had no intention of apologizing, Lily thought furiously; he just wanted his stuff!

"I'd rather come and pick them up personally," he insisted.

"What, are you afraid I'll hold back on a pair of your undershorts?" she retorted.

"You might like a few reminders of me," he declared arrogantly.

"I can assure you right now, Trent, your boxer shorts hold no pleasant memories for me," she blurted out before she realized what an embarrassing double entendre she had just come up with. She began to blush. Thank heaven Trent couldn't see that over the phone.

"If you want them, then come and get them," she barked into the phone. Oh no, she'd done it again!

"Is that an invitation?" he asked, and Lily could hear the amusement in his voice.

"No, it's an order." She slammed the receiver down. That man could certainly get under her skin. And the way he could turn things around! She realized that he had managed to manipulate the situation so that, instead of him having to ask to come over, she was demanding that he do so. And the worst part of it was that she could never tell when he was doing it; it just seemed to happen, as if she had no control over her own mind.

"Well," she began to talk to herself, "we'll just see what happens when he finally shows up!"

Half an hour later Lily was showered, dressed and made up. She had pulled her hair back in a severe bun, knowing that Trent hated it that way, and was wearing a high-necked green sweater and a matching long green pleated skirt. Green was Trent's least favorite color. Feeling sufficiently fortified against him, she sat on the sofa and waited for his arrival. It should come momentarily; it didn't take more than half an hour to take a cab from the Village to her place on the Upper East Side.

An hour later Lily was still waiting, and beginning to burn. Already she'd lost all the nails on her right hand to nervous biting and had made an appreciable impact on those of the left. Where was he? And then Lily fell prey to the kinds of worries women always had when their men were late: Had he been in a car crash? Had he been held up? Had he been run over by a truck? The more Lily thought about it, the more she decided that she hoped it was the latter. Wearing a body cast, Trent would be a much more manageable foe.

Finally, when she had only the little finger on her left hand to go to make the destruction of a second full handful of nails complete, the buzzer rang. Trent was downstairs in the lobby. Lily gave Adolfo her permission to let him up. She got the box of his things out of her bedroom and set it on the sofa, then stood in front of the door with her arms crossed and her feet wide apart and planted firmly on the floor. She supposed this was war.

When the doorbell rang she opened the door and let him in. He looked out of breath.

"I'm sorry I'm late, Lily. Something came up." He ran his fingers through his hair and then smiled winsomely at her.

Lily deduced immediately that he was going to show her his Prince Charming act. When she answered him, her voice was cool and steady. "That's all right. I hardly noticed," she lied. "I've been busy."

Before she had sat down to wait, she had turned on her typewriter and stuck a half-filled piece of paper in it so it would look as if she had been writing. He didn't have to know that she had actually spent the entire morning pining for him.

"Working?" he said as he moved closer to her.

She backed up. She didn't want him to get too close. Already she could feel her body's response to his nearness, and it was directly contradictory to the cool and collected message her mind wanted to send.

"Yes, I am." She walked over to her desk. "If you don't mind, I'm right in the middle of something. There's your box." She pointed to the sofa. "You can take it and leave."

"All right." He marched over to the box, picked it up and began to head back to the door.

Lily couldn't believe it. He was really going to leave! A little voice in her mind screamed at her: Forget your damn pride, Lily Lansden. Throw yourself at him. Grovel. Don't let that man out the door!

"Grovel?" she murmured to herself. Her little voice was going too far. Lily Lansden never groveled. She might plead or cajole, but grovel?

Trent's hand was on the doorknob. "Did you say something?" He turned and looked at her.

She felt the little hairs at the back of her neck stand up

and tingle, and her throat constricted just as it always did when he looked at her with his eyes turned to indigo.

"No," she replied. "I was just talking to myself, trying to figure this out." She began to type, but the letters came out as gibberish.

Trent turned back to the door, but he didn't open it; he remained standing before it as if there were something else he wanted to say.

"Uh, Lily . . ." he began.

"If you're wondering if all your things are there, you can check them," she said. If he was going to say something, she wasn't going to make it easy for him.

"I'll take your word for it." He put the box down and then came up behind her.

She covered up the page so he wouldn't see that she was so out of control that she couldn't even type. He put his hands on her shoulders and she could feel what little resistance she had left begin to melt. His touch was strong and possessive, and her shoulders instinctively warmed at the pressure of his long fingers. She slid out from beneath them, then stood and faced him.

"Was there something you wanted to say?"

He was actually stubbing the toes of his shoes against the carpet like a nervous schoolboy. Looking down, he finally said, "I've changed my mind."

"Oh." Lily knew what he meant, and her heart leapt in her throat, but damn it, she didn't want him to know how the relief at having him back was flooding through her system and making her head light and giddy.

"You don't want your things?" she managed to squeak sarcastically.

"Don't play games with me, Lily," he warned, glaring at her fiercely.

"You're accusing me of playing games?" Relief turned to anger. She couldn't believe the nerve of him. "One day you want me, then the next you don't. Then you come here and say you've changed your mind. I'm not the one who's playing games. You are, Trent." She pointed her finger at him accusingly.

"Things have changed," he insisted, and he swiped his hand at her outstretched finger. "Don't point at me," he ordered.

She put her hands on her hips. "Oh, you've decided not to be an arrogant, proud, stubborn son of a—" Lily caught herself just in time. She hated to swear. It was so unladylike. "Stubborn rat," she finished. "Is that what's changed?"

Trent turned and sat down on the sofa. He patted the cushion next to him. "Sit down, Lily."

"No," she stated firmly.

"Would you rather I made you sit down?" he threatened, his eyes sparking like sharp-faceted amethysts.

"I'd like to see you try," she dared.

He rose and headed over to her. He looked like he meant business.

Lily quickly conceded. "All right. I wanted to sit down anyway," she insisted.

They settled next to each other on the couch. But Lily kept a good three feet between them.

"Martin Gibson called this morning," Trent stated flatly.

"Oh," Lily answered with just the right amount of nonchalance. "That's nice."

"He likes my book. He wants to be my agent," Trent continued tersely.

"I don't see how that concerns me," Lily said.

"Things have changed," was all he said as he looked at her meaningfully.

"That's right, *things* have changed, but *you* haven't." Lily jumped up and stood before him, her anger rising to fever pitch.

"What do you mean?" Trent asked.

"I mean that all it takes is a call from Martin Gibson for you to decide that you've changed your mind and you want us to be . . ." She almost couldn't say it.

". . . lovers again. What if Martin Gibson calls back and tells you he's made a mistake, that it was someone else's book he liked so much and he'd mistaken it for yours? Then what? Will things change again? I'm not a Ping-Pong ball, Trent, and I refuse to be played with as if I am."

"You never cease to amaze me, Lily, with the ways in which you choose to deliberately misunderstand me," he said dryly.

"If Martin Gibson hadn't called, would you still be here?" she asked him, knowing that she had him with her question.

But he surprised her with his answer. "Yes," he said quietly. "I would."

"You would?" Deflated, Lily sank back down on the couch.

"I tried to call you last night, but your line was busy."

"I took the phone off the hook." So he had tried to get her last night. Why had she been so impulsive? She'd only hurt herself.

"I wanted to tell you something, but when I kept trying to get you and the line was busy for over an hour, I figured that you didn't want to talk to me. Then I figured that you were probably justified in not wanting to hear anything I said. But when I woke up this morning . . . I don't know . . ." He took her hand and his index finger traced a sensuous pattern in her palm. "I had to see you." He paused. Lily could see a flood of conflicting emotions washing across his face. "Remember when I told you that love has no pride?"

"Yes," she whispered as she rubbed his fingers with her own nervous ones.

"It's true, Lily. I was so wrapped up in my own pride, my own selfish feelings, that I was forgetting how much I love you. I let my own foolish pride stand between us." He squeezed her fingers. "What we have is too precious for us to let anything stand in its way."

"And if things don't go well with your book . . . ?"

She looked at him nervously. So much rested on his reply.

"I love you. That won't change." His hand was strong and firm, constant around hers.

"If that's how you feel, then why didn't you just say so?" Lily knew she was pressing him, but she had to be absolutely sure about Trent. She had to know that whether or not he was a success had nothing to do with his love for her. "If Martin Gibson had nothing to do with your decision, why did you bring him up?"

Trent looked slightly exasperated, but he knew he had to put all her doubts to rest, just as all his were gone. "When I saw you today, even in that ghastly green with your hair all tied up like a schoolmarm's, everything I planned to say just flew out of my mind. I felt like a bumbling schoolboy in front of the loveliest, sexiest girl of his dreams. I was so afraid that after what I'd said yesterday you wouldn't want to have anything to do with me."

"The thought had crossed my mind," she replied, removing his hand from hers and putting it in his lap. She wanted to be convinced that he loved her. He seemed so sincere about it. But how would she ever know that their reconciliation had nothing to do with Martin Gibson's offer?

"And now . . . ?" He put his other arm around her and pulled her close, crushing her breasts against his chest. She could feel the erratic beating of his heart.

"I don't know." She pulled away from him uneasily. "If only there was some way to prove what you're saying."

Now it was Trent's turn to pull away from her. "You want proof." He seemed insulted. "My word isn't good enough?" He shook his head. "Lily, what does love mean if not being able to trust someone?"

Lily looked at him and felt miserable. He was right. If she didn't trust him, then she didn't really love him. And she knew she loved him, so she had to trust him.

"How about a notarized statement?" Now he was getting sarcastic. "Or better yet, call Bev. I talked to her last night. I should have known a mystery writer would want a witnessed alibi."

Lily looked down and picked at the woolen threads of her skirt. "No, I believe you. Really I do. It's not necessary."

"Are you sure? You're not just saying that? We can't be doubting each other, Lily." His eyes were a clear, true purple. How could she doubt him when his eyes looked so clear and honest? She knew that she'd never ask Bev whether Trent had called. She loved him and she trusted him and she was wrong to suspect him.

Finally she looked up at him. "I'm sure. I love you. I'm glad you're here," she said softly. It was the simple, unadorned truth. Just the night they had spent apart had been enough to show her exactly how much she needed him and wanted him to be by her side. Always.

"Good!" Trent exclaimed, and then jumped to his feet.

Lily looked at him like he was crazy. Wasn't he even going to kiss her?

He glanced quickly at his watch. "I've got an appointment with Gibson in fifteen minutes, and I can't be late. We'll talk about this some more, okay? I'll come back here when I'm done." He raced for the door. "And take that ghastly green outfit off."

Lily followed him, slightly dazed by his eagerness to run out the door. "Don't I get a goodbye kiss?" she asked, and couldn't disguise the touch of wistfulness her request held.

"Of course." Trent leaned over her and pecked her chastely on the forehead. "There's more where that came from," he bantered, and then he was gone.

Lily leaned against the door, completely exhausted by the whirlwind that had preceded his departure.

"He certainly has a way with him," she murmured to the empty room.

* * *

A little while later Lily was standing in her walk-in closet, pushing clothing back and forth along the rod. She hadn't realized that she owned so many clothes that were green. She'd always liked green, especially the deep hunter and bottle greens, because they played so nicely against her ivory skin and pale blonde hair, but if Trent didn't like green . . . Well, today, at least, she'd humor him. Besides, if she wore something that pleased him, "that look" just might shine in his eyes. It was a look that meant only one thing, and that thing was nothing to be scoffed at.

Lily pushed aside a deep green silk blouse and found the teal blue silk dress she'd worn the day she'd met Trent. Maybe she should wear that for old times' sake; it had such pleasant memories attached to it. No, she finally decided, too corny. Instead she settled on a creamy yellow cashmere sweater and a tight-fitting navy blue skirt. She giggled as she threw them on the bed. If she was lucky, she wouldn't be wearing them for very long. She chose her lingerie carefully: an ivory lace bra and a matching teddy of silk edged with pale blue lace. She had to laugh out loud—she was deliberately getting dressed to be undressed. Life with Trent was a paradoxical state of affairs.

As she dressed she thought about Trent's news. So he was going to have Martin Gibson for an agent? It really was a wonderful thing for him. But how did that affect them? She'd been so tired last night, and so agitated this morning, that she really hadn't had a chance to let the full impact of most of what Trent had said the previous afternoon sink in. Some of it had been completely wrong and spiteful, but parts of it had been true.

For instance, when he'd said that he felt like her accessory . . . She supposed that from his point of view that must have been true. The week they'd spent together had been more a matter of his accommodating himself to her than her accommodating herself to him. They'd spent most of their time at her penthouse or visiting places that were familiar to her and fit into her life. They'd only stayed at his apartment once in all the time they were together. Lily could see now how that must have made Trent feel. He had had to make all the adjustments.

Well, from now on things would have to be different. She didn't really know that much about Trent's childhood. All he'd told her was that his father was a professor, and Lily knew that professors didn't make all that much money. His formative years must have been, not poor, but certainly not as well off as hers had been. Looking back, Lily could see that she had had a very fortunate life. Her father had been a wealthy banker, and her mother was descended from one of New York's founding Dutch families. She'd grown up with maids and cooks, finishing schools and debutante balls, and all the accoutrements of wealth. She'd been brought up to a certain kind of lifestyle. Even though she didn't go to some of the extremes that her friends did, with full household staffs and homes in the country and boats at the shore and all that nonsense, she still had a maid who came in two or three times a week, and she took many things, things that Trent would see as frivolous luxuries, totally for granted. If Trent was willing to rise above his feelings of male pride for the sake of his love for her, then she had to compromise, too.

Even though the future looked bright for him, there was always the possibility that he might not be as successful as she was. But love was more important than money or success, and mature love meant compromise and accommodation on both sides. She felt so filled with love for Trent that she could have sworn her heart was swelling in her chest. She and Trent were a pair now. They worked together. Whatever happened, bad or good, they would face it together.

"Well, how did it go?" was the first thing Lily said to Trent when she opened the door and let him in after his appointment with Martin Gibson.

He was so elated that he seemed to bounce across the carpet instead of striding with his usual long-legged gait. He grabbed her face in his hands and gave her a big, wet kiss.

"Wonderful. He's already sent the book over to an editor, and he's sure it will sell."

"Oh, Trent, that's wonderful," she squealed.

He left her side and went over to the window, where he stood looking down at Manhattan. Lily came up behind him softly.

"So the world's a pearl and you're holding it right in your hand, aren't you?" she whispered.

He turned, and his face was glowing with excitement. "I do feel that way. I've hoped for this for so long. But there's so much to do."

He left her and began to pace back and forth across the living room floor. "Once the book sells, I've got to meet the editor. I've probably got some revisions to do. I've got more meetings with Gibson to discuss terms and work out a contract. I'm going to have to find a lawyer." His pacing was taking on a frantic air.

"I've got a bottle of Fountaine champagne in the fridge. Would you like to make a toast and celebrate?" Lily asked.

Trent wheeled around and then stood stock-still. "Oh my God. Fountaine! I'd forgotten all about that." He ran his hands through his hair. "Lily, we've got to tell Fountaine that we're not married."

"Why?" she said, panic-stricken.

"You don't know what's going to happen, do you? Gibson seems to think I'm the literary find of the century. Even before the book comes out there's going to be all kinds of publicity. I can't be Lawrence Lansden anymore, Lily. Gibson seems to think Trent Daily's going to be a household word in a few more months."

"Oh." Things were going just a bit too fast for Lily to take them all in. It had never occurred to her that Trent's success would jeopardize their position with Albert, but it was obvious now that it would.

"How are we going to tell him? The commercial's all done. We can't back out now!" Lily was beginning to get scared.

"Look . . ." He came over to her side and took her in his arms. "We'll figure something out, but I can't do it now. I've got to get back to Gibson. We'll have dinner and talk, okay?" Already he was heading for the door.

"Okay," Lily said, and put a smile on her face. The last thing in the world Trent needed right then was a hysterical female. "I'll put on my thinking cap. We'll figure it out."

Trent flashed her a smile and then he was out the door. Lily flopped down on the couch. She'd think of some way to get them out of the mess they were in. She loved him, and she'd figure it out.

9

Even if she had been able to think of a way out of their situation with Albert Fountaine, Lily wouldn't have had a chance to tell Trent what it was. Between meetings with Gibson and appointments with his new lawyer and his new editor, who had snapped the book up immediately, Trent had little time for her. They hadn't even been able to have dinner the evening after they'd reconciled. Trent had had to write a short autobiographical blurb for Martin Gibson. Apparently his book was making a big stir in the literary community. Everyone who was anyone wanted to meet him.

That was why, on a Monday evening a week after Martin Gibson had taken him on as his newest client, Trent and Lily were on their way to a cocktail party at Gibson's penthouse suite.

"If I had any nails left I'd be chewing them," Lily remarked anxiously as their cab hurtled east toward Sutton Place.

"Are you nervous?" Trent asked, surprised. "You should be an old hand at these kinds of things."

"Well, yes, but . . ." Lily struggled for the composure that had been evading her ever since she'd dressed for the party. "Martin Gibson's parties have a tendency to have guest lists resembling *Who's Who in America*."

"You're in there, aren't you?" Trent chided her.

"One teensy paragraph. My claim to fame is that I'm a popular writer. Not exactly highbrow."

Trent raised his eyebrows, a visual pun on her phrase.

Lily continued. "I can't wait to see yours next year. At least a full page," she teased.

"Seriously, Lily." Trent changed the subject. "Are you really nervous?"

Lily plucked at her evening dress, a sophisticated black number with a short skirt of ruffled organza and a strapless top. "I hate to admit it, especially to you. . . ." In spite of their new togetherness, Lily still felt a bit of rivalry toward Trent. She supposed that would never go away. "But I am."

"Why? You're famous, aren't you?"

"But not the right kind of famous, Trent, and you know it. Everyone at that party is going to be . . . well, I'd hate to think what would happen to the cultural life of New York if a bomb were dropped on Martin Gibson's building tonight." She fiddled with her hair. She'd had it put up, and strands were already loosening from the elegant French braid.

Trent pulled her hands away. "Don't mess with your hair, Lily. It looks wonderful just as it is. And don't be nervous. You know, I wouldn't be surprised if you found some fans there tonight."

"More likely I'll be raked over the coals by some literary snob who'll accuse me of foisting junk on the American public."

"Well, if he does,"—Trent pulled her close and started kissing her, his lips hot against the soft skin of her neck—"let me know and I'll pop him one right in the kisser."

"I think that most literary discussions are resolved on a higher plane than that, Trent," Lily said, removing herself from his grasp. "And besides, I fight my own battles."

"You're not going to this party with your back up, are you?" Trent looked at her with a concerned expression.

"What are you saying?" She was highly insulted. "That I'm looking for trouble?"

"Well, from what you've been saying . . ." Trent scratched the side of his nose. "I wouldn't be surprised . . ."

"What do you think I'm going to do, challenge someone to a wrestling match?" she asked sarcastically.

Trent had to laugh. "I suppose that's a bit more democratic than just hauling off and popping someone on the nose."

"It's just, well . . ." Lily paused. She knew that Trent thought of her as someone who didn't have to worry about going to parties in penthouses, but this particular party almost terrified her. In the literary world, a mystery writer didn't have all that much status. She felt insecure, and that made her defensive. "Everything will be fine." She patted his hand. "I'll keep my temper in check; don't worry about me."

Trent clasped her hand, then raised it to his lips and gave it a quick kiss. "Well, here we are." The cab had pulled up to the sidewalk in front of Gibson's building.

On their way up in the elevator Lily continued to fuss with her hair. Next to her, Trent was the picture of composure. The only gesture he made which could have been even remotely considered nervous was when he straightened his cuffs so that just the right amount of white showed beneath his jacket sleeve.

As with most penthouses except her own, the elevator opened directly onto Gibson's apartment. A short hallway led to the living room of Gibson's suite. Lily had to pinch herself to keep from gasping out loud when they arrived in the main room.

Before her were so many famous faces that she couldn't even begin to count them. There was the writer who had made his mark exposing a major political scandal, standing next to an Amazonian brunette whose face was plastered on billboards across the country advertising the nation's largest cosmetics firm. There was the local gossip columnist who made his living telling slightly sanitized accounts of the comings and goings of the international jet set, sharing a cigarette with an Arab prince dressed in full desert regalia. A United States congressman who had once been a presidential hopeful was doing a wild free-form boogaloo with the previous year's winner of the ladies' Wimbledon championship and was in danger of stepping on the toes of this year's winner of the Nobel Prize for literature.

Lily turned to Trent and raised her eyebrows. "An intimate little gathering, isn't that what you said?" she whispered wryly. That was exactly how he'd said Gibson had described the party when he'd invited the two of them.

Trent laughed. "Do you think we've come to the wrong place?"

But before Lily had a chance to answer him, a dashing older man was shaking Trent's hand and welcoming him to the party. Lily recognized him from his pictures. It was Martin Gibson.

"So glad you could make my little do." He continued to shake Trent's hand as he winked at Lily. "And this must be the famous Ms. Lansden?"

Lily stuck out her hand. This was a greeting she hadn't expected.

He took her hand and shook it warmly. "Martin Gibson. I love your books. Read 'em like crazy. They go down like popcorn at the movies."

This Lily *had* expected, as if her books were something along the order of a fast-food hamburger or this year's latest fad, easily digested and completely disposable. Trent was looking at her, wondering what she was going to say to Gibson's inadvertent put-down.

"How refreshing," she said. "Usually I'm compared to potato chips."

Gibson did a double take. Lily knew that he couldn't be sure whether she was being sarcastic or self-deprecating. Trent didn't say anything; obviously he wasn't sure either.

"Well . . ." Gibson turned his attention back to Trent.

"There are simply scads of people I want you . . ." He paused, realizing his *faux pas*. ". . . you two to meet. Come on." He grabbed them both by their elbows and began to weave them in and out of the crowd.

Fifteen minutes later Lily realized that Gibson had been the epitome of politeness with his remark about her books being like popcorn. Half of the people she was introduced to acknowledged her with a kind of snobbish uneasiness, and the other half looked at her as if she were some unpleasant piece of fluff that the cat had had the nerve to drag in. Trent, on the other hand, was treated like visiting royalty—men simpered, and women practically threw themselves at his feet. The word certainly traveled fast in literary circles. Everyone wanted to be able to say that they had met Trent Daily before he'd become a famous writer, so they could lay claim to his discovery.

Finally Lily decided that she'd had enough and headed over to the bar in front of Gibson's spectacular view of the East River. She knew that she'd have to fortify herself in order to get through the evening since the last she'd seen of Trent, he'd been fending off the advances of a model. The last time Lily had seen the model had been in a fashion magazine, where she had been posing with a snake wrapped around her neck. The snake had been all she wore. Lily had never liked snakes, and she certainly didn't like the model. Her own possessive tendencies were making her feel as if she'd like to scratch the woman's eyes out, but she supposed that cat-fighting wasn't proper party behavior at Martin Gibson's.

She asked the bartender for a white wine spritzer, heavy on the wine, and then crossed to a corner that was empty compared to the rest of the room. People were standing shoulder to shoulder instead of chest to chest and back to back.

A man jostled against her and then turned to her with a smile and introduced himself. He was a writer for the most prestigious of the local papers.

Lily told him her name and his eyebrows rose. "You're a mystery writer, aren't you?" he asked.

Lily didn't know whether to deny it or not. Judging from the tone of the crowd so far, she thought it might be better to remain anonymous, but honesty won out and she told him that he was correct.

Suddenly he looked down at his glass. "Time for a refill," he said, and began to edge away. "But stay put. I'd like to talk to you." He looked at her meaningfully.

Lily watched as his back receded. He certainly had a novel way of dismissing her! She didn't believe for a minute that he had any intention of returning. She decided to hightail it for the nearest quiet place. At least wallflowers didn't run the risk of being insulted.

She wove her way through the crowd toward a hallway, and then opened the first door she came to. It was a guest room, she supposed; the bed was covered with furs and overcoats. She sat down on the bed and finished her wine, wondering what she was going to do next. She couldn't hide out all evening, but she didn't exactly feel like reentering the fray, either.

She had just about decided to go back out and get another glass of wine when she saw the bedroom door open. She hopped up and began to rummage through the furs. Whoever it was would think that she was trying to find her coat and she'd avoid the mortification of someone thinking that she was hiding from the rest of the party.

"Lily!" It was Trent. "You're not going home, are you?"

Lily had to use all her self-control to stop sarcastic words from bubbling out of her mouth, because her first instinct was to tell Trent that yes, she was leaving, since she didn't feel all that welcome.

"No," she said as she continued to rummage through the furs. "I'm just looking for my purse." She found it, then took out her lipstick and gave her lips a quick touch-up.

"Good. There's a man out there who wants to talk to you. He says you ran away from him."

"He's the one who ran away, not me," she said defensively. Lily figured Trent was referring to the reporter she had met earlier.

"Your skin is a little thin this evening," Trent said, and eyed her skeptically.

"My skin's as thick as a hippo's, Trent Daily," she answered angrily. "But unlike a hippo, I know when I'm being snubbed."

"You've got a fan out there, Lily!" he exclaimed.

"Oh, another popcorn eater?"

Trent looked at her with an annoyed expression on his face. "So Martin Gibson is a bit of a snob. He's not the only person here."

"Unfortunately, Trent, his *attitude* is about the only attitude here. In fact, it's a lot like yours was a month ago."

"Am I supposed to apologize for everyone out there? Or would you like me to go out and give a testimonial?" He got down on his knees. "Ah yes, once I was like you. I didn't believe in the mastery of Lily Lansden. Well, brothers and sisters, now I have seen the light." He raised his hands to the ceiling and shook them.

In spite of herself, Lily had to laugh. Trent looked like such a fool.

"Seriously, Lily," Trent said as he took her arm and led her to the door. "You changed my mind; why don't you change theirs?"

She looked at him, her eyes wide with disbelief.

"All right." He changed his tack. "At least come out and talk to your fan."

Before Lily even had a chance to agree with his suggestion, Trent was pushing her out the door. She was wading through some people, looking for the reporter she'd spoken with before, when she felt herself being jostled by a portly older man.

"Excuse me," he said, and then noticing, Lily supposed, her young, fresh face, he extended his hand. "Clement Spellford, critic for the *Review,*" he said with a touch of pomposity.

Lily assumed he could only mean the *Manhattan Review,* the literary circle's equivalent of the Bible.

"Lily Lansden," she replied, and held out her hand.

He took her hand at first, but when she said her name, he dropped it like a hot potato.

"Not the mystery writer?" he asked suspiciously.

"Yes," Lily said proudly. She was tired of being meek and apologetic about her profession. She had nothing to be ashamed of. "Yes, I'm Lily Lansden, the *famous* mystery writer."

"If you consider fame a worthy reward for the selling of poorly written junk to the ill-informed masses," he said snidely.

Lily gave him the once-over. This, she thought, was refreshing in its own obnoxious kind of way. At least he was saying exactly what he thought. She decided to take him on.

"Have you read any of my books, Mr. Spellford?" Whichever way he answered, Lily knew she had a quick retort for him.

"As a matter of fact, I have. Several. All absolutely ghastly." He said it as if it were the undeniable truth merely because it had originated in his mind and passed through his lips.

"One wasn't enough?" Lily baited him.

"I thought that, to be fair, I should read more than one." He raised his voice. Obviously he was going to make another pronouncement. "I consider reading mysteries a complete waste of time. As for writing them, I fear that they reduce the perpetrator to little more than trashmongering."

"I suppose you consider Sophocles a trashmongerer, then?" Lily asked boldly.

Spellford looked as if he were about to choke on his drink. "What?" he bellowed.

"What would you call *Oedipus Rex* if not a mystery? And what about Shakespeare? Did he also pander to the masses when he wrote *Macbeth?*"

"Dear girl, you're not comparing yourself to the great Bard, are you?"

"No, I'm too modest," she answered brightly. "But *Macbeth* is a mystery, just as surely as my books are. There was a murder, wasn't there? And a good part of the plot had to do with finding out who the killer was, didn't it? Do I need to say more?" She flashed him a dazzling grin and enjoyed watching him squirm.

"I'm afraid you'll have to say a great deal more. . . ." he answered evasively. Lily knew that she had him now.

"I don't mind if I do," she said. "As far as mystery writers go, they're quite a distinguished lot, Mr. Spellford. There's Edgar Allan Poe, T. S. Eliot, William Faulkner and Yeats. Would you like me to go on?" But she didn't wait for his permission. "I could reel off at least a dozen more Nobel and Pulitzer prize winners who were also mystery writers. How about Arthur Miller and John Steinbeck?"

Now that Lily was warming to her argument, her voice was getting louder. She noticed that several people in the near vicinity were nudging their companions and leaning closer to her and Spellford to get an earful of their heated conversation.

"Yes, Ms. Lansden, that all may be true, but you're not Eliot or Faulkner or the divine Edgar, and I doubt that fifty years from now anyone will even remember your books. They're tedious and eminently forgetable."

Lily leapt on his last statement. "So forgetable that you've remembered my name, and so tedious that you had to read several of them. If they hold no interest for you, why torture yourself with them?"

Spellford was looking distinctly uneasy now. The noise of the party had died down and all eyes were riveted on Lily and her portly companion.

"Well . . . ahem . . ." He had no answer.

"Mr. Spellford . . ." Lily drew herself up to her full height. "I don't pretend to be anything more than what I am—a storyteller. I deal in invention and surprise and suspense, just like any other novelist, except that I'm not afraid to entertain my reader. I don't need to weigh my plots down with a lot of overblown ideas and beat my readers over the head with a lot of philosophical hooey to get them to turn the pages. I grab them with my characters and my plots. I don't write trash; I just write what people want to read."

"That's just the point," Spellford finally had the presence of mind to answer. "You pander."

"And what's the use of a book that no one wants to read? Isn't that the whole purpose of writing? To get people to read?"

Now that Lily had an audience, she decided to move in for the kill. She was taking a risk with her next question, but if her suspicion was correct, she'd nail Spellford right to the floor. She turned to the crowd, who were now waiting on her every word.

"How many people here have read one of my books?" she asked.

She watched as people in the crowd looked at each other, wondering if it was all right to admit that they had indeed read her books. Trent was the first one to raise his hand. He held it high in the air and waved it slowly, like a victory flag. Standing next to him, Martin Gibson tentatively put his hand up to shoulder height and then waved it, too, as if beckoning all the other closet mystery readers in the room to join him and confess. Other hands began to pop up. Some waved along with Trent and Gibson, while some were adamantly still, as if they weren't all that sure they wanted to join the crowd but at the same time didn't want to be left out. Rings sparkled on slim fingers, and gold cuff links glittered at the ends of snowy white cuffs in the smoky party haze.

Lily waited until she was sure that everyone who was going to raise a hand had done so. Only a few held out, but it was obvious from the number of raised hands that she had a landslide vote in her favor. Slowly she turned to Clement Spellford, who seemed to have shrunk several inches in stature.

"I think we can call this discussion closed, don't you agree?" she said graciously.

His face had turned the color of a ripe plum, and his eyes were bulging like those of a surprised fish, but he conceded his defeat like a true gentleman. "I'm afraid I'm going to have to reconsider my stand, Ms. Lansden, in the face of such overwhelming evidence." He bowed to her and then exited, a defeated man.

Hands that had been raised in support before now fell and began to clap. It was the first time that Lily had ever received a standing ovation. Trent came to her side, gathered her up in his arms and gave her a resounding kiss, to the cheers of everyone present.

Martin Gibson came over to them and slapped Lily on the back. "If I hadn't seen it with my own eyes, I wouldn't have believed it," he said, shaking his head.

"It is rather astounding, isn't it?" Trent said, and looked at her lovingly.

Lily moved away from his embrace. "Are you that surprised that there are so many mystery readers here?" she asked. "Or are you just surprised that they admitted to it?"

Trent looked at Gibson, and they both burst into laughter. Lily looked back and forth between the two of them. "Is there something here that I'm missing?"

Trent led her away from the crowd and over to a quiet corner. Gibson followed.

"Lily, we're laughing because we can't believe that someone got the best of Clement Spellford," Trent said.

"You see," Gibson chimed in, "Spellford's like that little boy in the cereal commercial. He doesn't like anything. Most of the writers here are scared to death of him. He's got his own little monopoly on what is and isn't 'great literature.'" Gibson raised his hands and pretended to make little quotation marks around his last words.

"So," Trent finished Gibson's thoughts for him, "no one here would dare to tell him off. But you did. That makes you a bit of a heroine in this neck of the woods."

"I had no idea." Lily began to tremble just a bit. "He didn't seem all that fearful to me," she said weakly.

"He's the man we all love to hate," Gibson said. "You've done us all a great service, Lily. Spellford's going to have a hard time now being so pompous about his likes and dislikes."

Lily sighed. "I feel a little bit like Dorothy when she set her house down on the Wicked Witch of the West."

Trent and Gibson laughed.

"That's not a bad analogy, Lily," Trent said.

"Yes," Gibson chortled. "If only we had a pair of ruby slippers for you."

"I'll settle for a drink," she said wearily. She was beginning to feel the enormity of what she'd just done. Thank goodness she hadn't known she was doing it while it was going on.

"I'll get it," Gibson piped up. "I can't wait to see what everyone has to say!"

But before Gibson could return with her drink, Lily was being besieged by well-wishers on every side, pressing drinks into her hand and kisses on her cheek. They were all thrilled at her conquest of Spellford. And every one of them demanded a personally autographed copy of her new book when it came out. They figured, Lily supposed, that if they hadn't read her yet, it was time to do so; anyone who could get the best of Clement Spellford had to be a force to be reckoned with.

Finally, after most of the well-wishers had come and gone, Trent turned to her. "How does it feel to be the life of the party?" he teased.

"Tiring," she said, and pressed her hand to her forehead. "But I'm a little worried."

"Why?" Trent must have known that she wanted to leave. He pushed her in the direction of the bedroom so she could retrieve her fur.

"Well," she said, "I feel a little guilty. This was supposed to be your night, not mine."

"It *was* my night," Trent insisted as he closed the bedroom door behind them. "And it was your night, too. It was *our* night." He pulled her close to him.

"Then we shared it?" she asked breathlessly as his lips hovered just millimeters away from her own.

"We shared it," he said, and then dipped his head even lower to plant a fiery kiss on her mouth.

She melted into his warm arms and felt the tingles that always accompanied his touch flutter up and down her spine.

He pulled away momentarily. "What do you say we go home and celebrate?" he asked, and the twinkling in his eyes gave her a good indication of the exact manner in which he intended to make merry.

Lily sat before her vanity brushing her hair, while in the mirror, she watched Trent lounging on the bed in his bathrobe, watching her. She had never known, until she fell in love with Trent, the pleasures of ritual. Every evening before they succumbed to the delights of their bed, Trent watched while she performed her toilette. It had become a preliminary to their lovemaking. And every morning they had another ritual. One of Trent's first gifts to her, after the silk nightgown, had been an automatic coffee maker with a timer. They began their breakfast in bed, sipping coffee in between kisses.

Lily caught Trent's eye in the mirror and smiled. "You watch me like a cat," she teased.

"If you don't get into this bed immediately, I'm going to attack you like a cat," he said, and crouched on all fours, growling like a fierce lion.

"All right, all right." She jumped up and rushed over to the bed. He grabbed her and turned her on her side to face him, then pressed himself against her. She could feel his hardness against her thigh.

"Now I'm going to make you purr like a cat," he whispered. His breath was warm and intoxicating against her ear. He began to stroke her thighs, lifting up her nightgown to get at the warm flesh beneath.

Lily forced her breath against her palate in a reasonable approximation of a purr. "I'm purring," she said.

"You won't scratch, will you?" He nipped at her shoulder where the strap of her gown had fallen away.

"Not unless you want me to," she answered, loving his touch.

"Save it till later," he growled fiercely, and then pulled her even tighter against himself.

His hands reached down and began to massage her legs from her knees to the point where her thighs met and then he dipped his fingers into the place where she longed to be touched. His touch was sure and confident. Now that he knew how to arouse her to the point of senselessness, he was relentless in his desire to bring her just to the point of fulfillment and then leave her there at the brink, aching for more.

"Trent, please," she begged.

He didn't bother to answer her plea. His hands moved up her body and cupped her breasts in his palms, while his fingers tugged and then softly caressed their hard peaks. His lips were hot against her neck, biting and then sucking the tender flesh and sending chills down her back. Her whole body was awash with desire. She couldn't imagine wanting him any more than she already did.

He pulled his hands away from her body and ripped off his robe. At the feel of his flesh against her own, Lily's nerve endings cried out for release. But he refused to grant her what she craved. He nudged her legs apart and made teasing forays toward the center of her desire, but always he withdrew before completing their union. She moaned and writhed beneath him. How could he torment her this way? She felt as if she were a flower being coaxed into bloom, a sea anemone unfurling and billowing in hot tropical waters, a ripe piece of fruit being bitten into for the first time. Trent's hands reached down and parted her thighs even further as he withdrew for one final moment and then completed the union he had obviously been longing for as much as she had. She gasped with pleasure.

Slowly he moved against her until she began to respond to his rhythm and answered his thrusts with her own movements. For what seemed like hours, they lay together like that, undulating like waves rippling across fine, silken sand. Lily was delirious with desire. Trent put his hand up to her mouth to caress her lips in a symbolic kiss, and she sank her teeth lightly into the flesh of his fingers, and then took one into her mouth and caressed it with her tongue.

"Oh, Lily," he moaned.

"Trent, please." She wrapped her legs around his hips and drew him even more deeply into her. The feeling was more exquisite than she could ever have imagined. A sharp sigh escaped her lips.

And then the sigh turned into an exclamation of surprise. Slowly and surely, Trent was bringing her even closer to the brink of abandon. She grasped his back with her fingers and dug them into his hard flesh. Their movements took on a quality of frenzy. There was no turning back now. With a masterful thrust, Trent brought her to the edge and beyond just as he crossed over himself. Her body surged with sensation, rippling from head to toe, tossed like a piece of storm-driven flotsam on a sea of desire.

10

Lily awoke to the smell of coffee. In fact, she awoke to a coffee cup hovering beneath her nose and, above the cup, Trent's smiling face.

"Rise and shine, my little heroine," he teased.

Lily sat up and sipped some coffee. It was very light, just the way she liked it. "Mmmmm," she said.

"Here's the paper. I've already been through it." Trent smiled at her again, but this time his grin held a touch of something else besides his usual morning-after happiness. Lily was too groggy to comment on it.

He handed her a copy of the morning tabloid.

"What's this?" she asked. Usually he bought both what she called the "real paper" for her and the tabloid for himself. He claimed that he got all kinds of story ideas from its contents.

"They were all out. But I think you'll find this more interesting." Now his face was deadpan. "Turn to page eight."

Lily opened the paper and found that she was staring at the local gossip column. It was usually filled with news about visiting celebrities, local politicians and the latest society parties. This time her name, in boldface type, jumped off the page.

"Oh no!" she exclaimed.

"Read it," Trent suggested.

Lily scanned it quickly. It was a rundown of Martin Gibson's party. After a list of the most notable guests there was a long paragraph, and the paragraph was all about her showdown with Clement Spellford. It ended with the columnist calling her the literary circle's "newest darling."

"Darling?" she ejaculated. "Is that what I've become?"

"Don't be surprised if your next book gets front-page treatment in the book review section," Trent joked. "You've performed a vital service, Lily. You'll be reward-ed for it."

She laughed. "Do you think they'll compare me to Shakespeare?"

"Well, I don't think they'll go that far." Trent laughed along with her. "Maybe just Faulkner or Poe."

"Not bad company," she mused. Then she read further. "Hey!" she yelled. "You're in here too!"

Trent beamed. " 'Up-and-coming writer Trent Daily.' I know. It's great, isn't it? What a combination: up-and-coming and newest darling. It's unbeatable."

"What's a 'woosome twosome'?" That was what the columnist said she and Trent were.

"I think that means"—Trent took her coffee cup away from her and pushed her down on the bed with his other hand—"we're lovers," he growled, and attacked her neck with his lips.

Lily giggled. "What a funny way of saying it." She let Trent continue to ravish her neck, and then something struck her.

"Holy cow!" She sat up quickly, as if one of Trent's kisses had ignited a fuse and she was being launched into the air.

"What is it?" Trent grumbled. He obviously didn't like being interrupted so abruptly in the middle of his seduc-tion.

"Albert Fountaine." It was all she needed to say.

Trent scratched his head. "You're right. I was so pleased at seeing our names together that I didn't even think of it."

"What's he going to think?" Lily moaned.

"This does tend to complicate things." Now Trent scratched his chin.

"He's going to think I'm having an affair with you!"

"Well, you are, aren't you?" Trent grinned wickedly.

"Yes, but you're my husband Lawrence." Lily followed through logically. "But you're not really, you're Trent Daily, and we're having an affair . . . but . . . oh, brother." The absurdity of the situation was making her head spin.

"Married people don't tend to have affairs with each other, do they?" Trent mused. "Usually they choose someone else."

Lily flung the covers aside and jumped out of bed. She was stark naked. She ran to the bathroom, plucked her robe off the hook on the back of the door and ran back into the bedroom. She was fluttering around like a chicken with its head cut off.

"Maybe he won't see it," Trent offered.

"Oh no." Lily began to pace. "He'll see it. He has this service that sends him clippings every week about anything and anyone connected with the winery. He'll see it, all right."

"Well, you knew we had to work something out along these lines," Trent said.

"I know, but you've just been so busy, and I've been trying to keep up with you *and* work on my book, and we haven't had much of a chance to discuss it. I thought we'd have more time. Now we don't. We've got to move on this one right away." Lily had stopped pacing. Now she was practically running back and forth, the hem of her robe whipping around her ankles.

Trent reached out and grabbed her in midflight. "Will you please slow down? You're making me dizzy." He pulled her down onto the bed.

Lily stared at him. He didn't seem all that upset. In fact, he looked as cool as a cucumber. "Doesn't this bother you?" she asked.

"No, not really," he said evenly.

"It bothers me. I hate to be caught in a lie," she wailed.

"Are you afraid your nose is going to grow?" Trent yanked on her nose. "It's such a lovely nose, I don't blame you for being upset."

"Oh, you." Lily slapped his hand away.

"Are you more upset by the fact that you lied, or by the fact that you got caught?" he asked gently.

Lily considered his question. Like most of Trent's observations, it cut straight through to the heart of the matter. He was right. When she'd begun this deception she should have considered the consequences of exposure. She'd just never thought it would actually happen.

"That I got caught, I suppose," she murmured. "I better call Bev."

"I already have," Trent said, surprising her.

"What did she say?"

"Her solution to the problem was very simple. She suggested that we get married."

Lily stared at him open-mouthed. Was this a proposal?

"Either that or be sued for fraud."

"You have a wonderful way of putting things," Lily said dryly. "Marry me or go to jail."

"What's your answer?" he asked.

He had to be kidding! Did he seriously expect her to marry him just to save herself from being thrown into the pokey? Where was the romance? Where was the gentle proposal? He wasn't even on his knees!

"You're a true romantic, Trent," she said sarcastically as she headed for the bathroom.

"Well, what's your answer?" He got up and followed her.

"Can't a person go to the bathroom in peace?" she snapped. If she had dreamt of Trent proposing to her before—and she had—it definitely hadn't been in this manner. There had been candles and moonlight and, if not roses, at least a few flowers scattered about.

"I'll talk to Bev and let you know," she said, and slammed the door in his face.

"Well, you better decide soon," he yelled through the door. "I just might change my mind."

A few minutes later she heard him leave the room, and then she heard the front door slam shut behind him. She sat down on the edge of the bathtub. Now she was really in a pickle, because she knew that even if she did talk to Bev, she would only offer Lily the same solution she had offered to Trent. And she supposed that if she had to choose between the two alternatives, jail—or public humiliation at the very least—and marriage, she'd choose marriage. Prison uniforms were so unattractive.

Bev looked up from behind her desk, surprised. Lily had barged into her office without even bothering to let Bev's secretary announce her. Lily was too impatient to see her to bother with ordinary office etiquette. She threw the paper down on Bev's blotter.

"Have you seen this yet?" she moaned.

"Only heard. Haven't had a chance to get my own copy yet." Bev opened the paper and thumbed through it until she got to the gossip page. She began to laugh.

"I don't see why everyone thinks this is so damn funny!" Lily exclaimed.

"Don't you like being the literary circle's newest darling?" Bev asked.

"It's not that, and you know it," Lily replied firmly.

"You're jealous of Trent because he's up-and-coming?" Bev teased.

"Bev Simmons, you know exactly why I'm here."

"It's the 'woosome twosome.' I know." Bev flipped the newspaper shut. "It is rather unusual to be having an affair with the man you're supposedly married to," she mused. "But then, Trent's an unusual man," she finished.

"Unusual and aggravating," Lily stated.

"Well, if Albert sees this—" Bev began.

"Of course he's going to see this," Lily butted in. "Even though he's upstate at the winery, he has this clipping service—"

Now Bev interrupted *her*. "He's not upstate. He's here at the Waldorf. He told me last week that he'd be here all this week."

"Oh, brother," Lily moaned. "It's even worse than I thought. He probably already knows!"

"I don't think so," Bev said. "If he did, believe me, he would have called. It's not the kind of news you hear and keep quiet about. He's invested a lot of money in you and Trent."

"Don't remind me," Lily groaned. The situation was going from the worst to worse than the worst.

"Did Trent tell you what I suggested?"

Lily eyed her wearily. "Yes. It was a charming proposal. I get to choose between marriage and jail. I don't know which one is the more unpleasant."

"Jail would probably be a trifle tiring, Lily. Why don't you choose marriage?" Bev egged her on.

Lily had figured something out on her way over in the cab. "What the two of you fail to realize is that the problem isn't merely that we're not married. The problem is also that there *is no* Lawrence Lansden. If I marry Trent, that only solves half the problem. What happens to Lawrence?"

Bev leaned forward. "An interesting conundrum, Lily." Was she mocking her, or was she taking her seriously? Lily couldn't tell. "What do we do with Lawrence?"

"Kill him," Lily said simply.

If Bev had been mocking her, Lily had just snapped her out of it. "Kill Trent?"

"No," Lily said. "Kill Lawrence. There's this wonderful poison that the South Americans use. One drop and the victim keels over within minutes. Not too painful, either."

"I hope you know what you're talking about, Lily, because I'm completely lost."

"I'll explain. All we have to do is say that Lawrence died. Maybe I had this display of deadly drugs in the apartment, like some mystery writers have collections of guns or instruments of torture, and poor dim-witted Lawrence just happened to gulp one of the exhibits down by mistake. He's dead. Then it's all right for me to be seen with Trent."

"But, Lily . . ." Bev was looking at her as if she had just gone around the bend right before her eyes. "How do you deal with the fact that Trent will look exactly like Lawrence?"

"Twins." That was easy.

"With different last names?"

"Half brothers?" Lily felt as if the solid ground she had once thought was so firmly established beneath her feet was beginning to shift. Was the possibility of marrying Trent in fact driving her around the bend?

"Lily, if you wrote that idea in a book, I'd toss it right out the window. Accept it. You have no choice but to marry Trent."

"But that still doesn't explain—" she began.

"Look, you're in a no-win situation. At least if you marry Trent, Albert can still use you two as a couple. Maybe he'll be a little miffed that you lied to him—and come to think of it, I don't get out of this scot-free either; I set up the deal—but anyway, maybe he'll be a little miffed, but he probably won't sue you. The commercial hasn't been aired yet. There's time to change Lawrence Lansden's name to Trent Daily."

"I knew you'd side with him," Lily said heatedly.

"Honey . . ." Bev came over to where Lily was slumped in the chair and put her arms around her shoulders. "Have you ever thought that Trent might actually want to marry you?"

"Then why doesn't he say so?" she demanded.

"Maybe he's scared. Maybe you're scared, is more likely, and he knows it," Bev said.

"I'm not scared," Lily snapped back without even thinking, even though on further reflection she knew that there was a grain of truth in Bev's statement.

"Come on, Lily, I know you." Bev stood in front of her with her arms crossed.

"All right. I'm a little scared. My track record hasn't been all that good." She was thinking of James.

"Lily, James doesn't count. He didn't love you, and you didn't really love him. You only thought you did. Trent loves you. I know that for a fact."

"How do you know?"

"He calls me practically every day, Lily. He's always asking me how to do this, or how to do that, so he'll please you. He loves you more than anything. Isn't that enough?"

"I don't know. You see . . ." Lily got up and began to pace back and forth across the carpet. "There are our careers. What if he flops with his book? What if I flop with my books? It seems as if so much depends on whether or not he's a success. If he isn't, I just don't know. . . ." She stopped when she realized what she was saying. She had thought she'd put all those doubts behind her, but here they were, popping up again. Perhaps there was only one way to put them to rest for good. She had to ask Bev the question she had resolved never to ask.

"You say that Trent calls you all the time. Did he call you the night we got into an argument after the Coliseum show?" Lily's voice was quiet, but clear.

"Oh, brother." Bev smiled while she said it. "The man was distraught. He felt like such a fool. He thought he'd lost you for good when your line was busy all night. He figured you'd never talk to him again, but I assured him that you would, once you heard what he had to say."

"What did he have to say?" Lily asked meekly.

"That he loved you and he didn't give a damn about your being more successful than he was or his being more successful than you were." Bev paused for emphasis. "He made it very clear."

It was everything that Lily wanted to hear. And yet, she had one final doubt, a doubt only a woman would have. "What if all this success goes to his head? What if he wants to run around with starlets or models or frail, anemic poets?"

Bev laughed, but in between chuckles she threw Lily a piercing glance. "You think you can't hold on to him?"

The question caught Lily up short. "I guess that's it, isn't it? The success thing is really just a screen for what's really on my mind. I'm afraid that our love won't last. It didn't last with James."

"I repeat: That wasn't love. You know it as well as I do. Put the past behind you, where it belongs. You have a wonderful future with Trent. Why can't you see that?"

Lily looked at Bev. Was she being a fool? Was she being a coward? Why couldn't she accept Trent's love and just go on from there?

"It's so risky," she said.

"You get up in the morning, Lily, and you put your foot out the door and it's risky. Anything can happen. Does that stop you from going outside?"

"No," she said in a tiny voice.

"Life is risky, Lily. You can't get around that. But you can say to yourself that even if it *is* a risk, you can still enjoy life to the fullest. Take a chance. Marry the man. He's so much in love with you. The only risk you take is that he'll love you to death."

Lily blushed. She knew what it was like to be loved to death by Trent. It wouldn't be a bad way to go. She smiled. She walked over to Bev and hugged her. "Thanks," she said.

"I want my favorite writer to be happy. If it means pounding a little sense into her stubborn head every once in a while, it's worth it."

Lily looked over Bev's shoulder and saw the newspaper lying on the desk. "What about Albert?"

Bev walked over to her desk, picked the paper up and handed it to Lily. "I suggest you show it to him and level with him. Use that Lansden charm. I get the feeling that you'll have him eating out of your hand by the time you're done. He'll be wondering why he didn't think of the whole thing himself. The story does have a certain amount of publicity value." Bev eyed her sagely.

"You're right. The hired husband who turns into the real husband. It's kind of funny, when you think about it."

"I knew that one of these days your sense of humor would reappear," Bev chided her gently.

"He's at the Waldorf?" Lily asked.

"Suite 909."

"I'll let you know how it works out," Lily yelled over her shoulder as she dashed out of Bev's office. But she knew, just as she knew that Bev knew, that everything would work out just fine.

The cab inched through the usual lunchtime traffic snarl in midtown Manhattan on its way to the Waldorf. Lily fumed in the back seat. She thought that it would probably have been smarter to walk—she would have gotten there faster, and she could have used up some of the nervous energy that was making her twine her hair nervously around her fingers.

"Can't you go any faster?" she prodded the cabby.

He turned around and looked at her skeptically. "If you were in a hurry, lady, you should have taken a helicopter."

Trust a New York cabby to come up with a snappy answer. Lily sat back in the seat and thought about what she was going to say to Albert Fountaine. She decided not to shilly-shally around the issue. She'd just spill the beans right off, and then mop them up as charmingly as possible. Albert seemed to be the type of man who appreciated forthrightness.

Since he seemed to be such a font of wisdom, Lily decided to ask the cabby for some advice. "I've got a problem," she said to the back of his neck.

"Oh yeah?" he said. "What—you don't have any money and you want me to take you there for free, right?" Cabbies always tended to look on the practical side of things.

"No, it's a little more complicated than that."

"Well, go ahead. The advice is free."

Lily quickly ran down her situation in as simple a manner as possible. When she was finished, the cabby didn't say a word. Maybe he thought there was more to it.

"Well, what do you think?" Lily asked.

"That's not a problem. That's a disaster."

"I'm not asking for your opinion, I'm asking for some advice. What should I do?"

"Have you thought of leaving the country? Want me to take you to Kennedy Airport instead?"

Lily pondered his solution for half a minute, and then decided that it was rather impractical.

"I don't speak any foreign languages."

"Guess that rules that out. Well, you know what they say: You can fool some of the people some of the time, and all of the people all of the time, but not some of the people . . . Wait . . . You can fool some of the people all of the time, and all of the people . . . No, that's not right. . . . You can—"

"Enough," Lily commanded. At the rate he was going, she'd have to drive to the North Pole with him until he got it right.

"How about, Honesty is the best policy?"

"I was hoping for something a little more illuminating than that," Lily complained good-naturedly. Obviously he had no solution to her problem, but at least he was keeping her entertained until she reached her destination.

"Lady, I'm a cab driver, not a lawyer." He ran his third consecutive red light and pulled up in front of the Waldorf. "Here we are."

Lily tossed a ten-dollar bill over the divider between them. "Keep the change," she told him.

"Hey, thanks, lady. Look, you want my real advice, I'll give it to you. Marry the guy. You don't look like the type who'd do too well in a prison cell."

Lily hopped out of the cab. "Thanks. I think you talked me into it," she said dryly. She ran into the Waldorf's lobby, then headed for the elevator and took it up to Fountaine's floor. It was the moment of truth.

She buzzed Albert's door and he answered shortly.

"Lily!" He looked glad to see her. "I wasn't expecting you."

Now that she was facing him, her resolve seemed to dwindle to nothing. "Oh, I thought I'd pay a friendly call," she said. The little voice in her mind was beginning to wail: "Tell him, Lily. Tell him the truth, you yellow-bellied coward."

"Can I get you something? A drink?" Albert asked graciously.

"I'd love one." She sat down in a chair in the living room and tucked her feet up under her nervously.

"Sherry? A little white wine?" Albert offered her the traditional ladies' drinks.

"Do you have any bourbon?" she asked.

He nodded.

"Give it to me straight."

Albert looked at her, but was too much of a gentleman to say what Lily knew he must have been thinking. Straight bourbon at twelve noon? He had to know that something was wrong.

He handed Lily a short glass filled halfway with the amber liquid. She did a pretty good approximation of a Mississippi River gambler, downing the whole glass with a quick snap of her wrist.

"More?" he asked, amazed.

"No, that's fine. So how are things, Albert?" Again she was taking the coward's way out.

"Pretty good. The convention really stirred up a lot of business."

"Why are you down here?" she asked. Anything to keep the conversation going on a completely harmless level.

"Finalizing the airtimes for the commercial. We're blowing a lot of money on prime time. It's going to make a big splash."

That was the last thing in the world Lily wanted to hear. But she supposed that now was the time to begin to touch on the issue of why she'd come.

"You haven't looked at the paper today, have you, Albert?"

"No, I never read the paper. I watch the news on TV; it's a lot easier. My service sends me whatever articles I absolutely have to see, so I leave that to them and stick to the six o'clock news."

If she could have, Lily would have blurted out, "Good, don't ever read the paper," and run for the door. But she couldn't. As the expression went, the time was now.

"Uh, Albert . . ." she began as she twisted her legs into a pretzel shape beneath her. "There's something I have to tell you. . . ."

"Go ahead, dear girl." He settled himself in a chair opposite her own and waited for her to continue.

"You know my husband, Lawrence?" The ball was finally rolling.

"A charming young man. Yes, of course I know Lawrence." He was looking at her as if, for the life of him, he couldn't figure out what she was getting at.

Well, this is it, folks, Lily thought to herself, and then made the plunge. "He's not my husband." She closed her eyes. She couldn't stand to see the look she knew would be on Albert's face. She prayed that he was an even-tempered man and would only give her a tongue-lashing instead of chucking her out the door.

Silence filled the room until finally he broke it. "I know."

Lily's eyes popped open. "You know?" How could he possibly know?

"I've known for weeks. I've known since that day we filmed the commercial. Or, rather, I learned about it the night before."

"But . . . but . . ." Lily spluttered. "How did you know? Who told you?"

"Why, Trent, of course." He said it as if it should be obvious.

"Trent told you?" Lily squeaked. Now she was sure she was going to go to jail. She could see no option before her other than to kill Trent!

11

I thought you knew I knew!" he exclaimed.

"I didn't know! No one tells me anything!" Lily's head was spinning. Why had Trent told Albert? Why hadn't Trent told her that he'd told Albert? Why hadn't Albert backed out of the deal when he'd found out?

"I thought we were all just pretending, just for the fun of it. Trent told me that night when you two worked on the script together. Although, I have to tell you, Lily, that he didn't tell me willingly. I had to pry it out of him."

"You suspected?"

"Of course. Did you think I wouldn't? No happily married couple ever 'darlings' and 'loveys' half as much in a year as you and Trent did in the first hour we were all up there. You two were just too perfect. It was glaringly obvious."

So much for the "great deception," Lily thought to herself. It was a good thing she had a career as a writer; she'd never make it as an actress.

"But why did you keep us, then? Why didn't you break the contract?"

"What? And lose you and Trent? You were perfect together once you wrote your own script, just like I knew you'd be. And besides, who says you really have to be married just because you're married on television? I can think of one instance—I won't mention any brand names, Lily—where two people who aren't married pretend that they are, and it sure doesn't stop the

American public from buying truckloads of cameras. No, you and Trent were perfect for the job. Why let a few technicalities stand in the way?"

"Then I don't have to marry Trent . . ." Lily thought out loud.

"Pardon?"

"It doesn't matter to you if we're not really married?" she restated herself.

"Not in the least," he said with a shrug of his shoulders. "As long as you two sell a lot of champagne for me, you can have whatever marital status you prefer."

"But Trent told me, and Bev told me . . ." Lily murmured. Obviously there was a conspiracy afoot.

"What did he tell you?"

"That if I didn't marry him, you'd sue us for breach of contract," she blurted out.

Albert merely laughed, a deep hearty laugh. "That certainly is the most novel proposal I've ever heard. What did you tell him?"

"I said no, of course," she replied with all the dignity she could muster.

Albert pondered her answer while he stroked his beard. "I wouldn't do that, Lily."

"Why?" Albert had to be in on the conspiracy too. The whole world was against her.

"Because I hate to think of what other stunts Trent will dream up just to get you to the altar. If you value your life, dear girl, and you want a little peace and quiet for a change, I suggest you marry the man. He seems particularly driven to make you his wife."

"Is that what you think?"

"Of course. It's obvious, isn't it? Ah, Lily." He rose and came to her side. "Love *is* blind, isn't it?"

"Addlebrained is more like it," she muttered beneath her breath.

"Let me tell you something, Lily. I got the biggest kick out of you and Trent while we were shooting that commercial. It was truly charming to see two people who were supposedly married falling in love right before my eyes."

"Is that what we were doing?" she asked, but it was a rhetorical question and she knew it. She knew that she loved Trent, and she knew that he loved her. It was simple.

"Lily, if you two don't get married, well . . . why disappoint an old man?" He beamed at her.

"If you put it that way, I don't see how I can refuse." Lily's eyes shone up at him.

"Make it a big splashy wedding. And serve lots of Fountaine champagne." His eyes twinkled back at her.

"Albert, we'll bathe in it."

"Whatever you want. Just make sure you invite me."

It was time to track Trent down. Lily hopped into another cab and headed down toward the Village. When she got to his apartment she buzzed, but there was no answer. If he wasn't there, where could he be? She checked out a couple of coffee shops that she knew he frequented, but he wasn't at any of them.

She hopped another cab and went back up to her penthouse. Maybe he'd be there. If he wasn't, she'd just wait until he got in touch with her. At least this way she'd have some time to plot her revenge. He couldn't trick Lily Lansden and get away with it!

When she got up to her place and walked in the door, she saw that she was going to have to wing it. Trent was lounging on the couch.

He turned his head casually as she walked in the room. "Hello, Lily."

"Hello, Trent," she said calmly. She'd learned by now that it was always best to remain perfectly calm at the outset. Sooner or later he'd have her reduced to hysteria, but at least she could begin with half a head on her shoulders.

"How'd it go with Bev?" he asked, as if he didn't know.

"Just fine," she said, and sank into an easy chair opposite him. She avoided his eyes and concentrated instead on plucking at the upholstery.

"What did she say?" Lily looked up. Trent's eyes were like dark amethysts with onyx centers.

"Trent, who has the purple eyes, your mother or your father?" Lily had always wondered about that. Now was as good a time as any to find out.

"Neither," he said impatiently. "My mom's are blue, and my dad's are brown."

"Aren't genes wonderful?" she mused abstractedly. She was going to make him squirm for a while. He deserved it.

"What did Bev say?" he demanded again.

"What do you think she said? You talked to her, didn't you?" Lily was stalling for time, hoping that a brainstorm would hit. Suddenly it did. "She did have something interesting to add, though."

"Oh, what's that?"

She knew that Trent wasn't expecting any additions. He thought he had her cornered. "She says that, actually, I'm not the one who's in danger of going to jail."

"What?" Trent shouted and jumped up.

"Yes." Lily remained seated, trying to appear as calm and as rational as possible. "She says that I'm not the one who pretended to be anything I'm not. You're the one who assumed a false identity. So you'll be the one who goes to jail."

"Bev never said that!" he stated vehemently.

Now she had him! "How would you know?"

"Because we talked this whole thing through—" He stopped. Lily knew that he knew that if he went any further he would only incriminate himself more than he already had.

"Oh, and just what did you and Bev talk through?" she said sweetly.

"Nothing." He sat back down on the couch.

"Albert seemed to feel the same way," she added.

"He did?"

Lily could see that Trent was genuinely perplexed. His scheme had gone awry, and he obviously didn't like it one bit. He didn't like being the one who was teased. It was an unfamiliar role. But Lily enjoyed watching him trying to figure his way out of the mess. She could almost hear the gears whirling in his head. But she knew that he was getting nowhere.

"Albert doesn't *really* want to sue you," she said, and waited for his reaction, but there was none. "But he doesn't see how he can avoid it. It's the principle of the thing, you see." She dared to look up into his eyes. Now they looked as if they were on fire. She figured that she had better finish up fast and then run for cover. He looked as if he were about to explode.

"So Albert suggested that if I could find it within the depths of my heart to take pity on you . . ." She realized that she was playing it for all it was worth, and it made her recklessly giddy. "I could marry you. That is, if I don't want to see you behind bars."

"Oh, is that what he said?" Trent stood and began to advance toward her. His hands twitched at his sides. Lily remembered that she had a neck, and that it was a rather delicate one at that. She hopped up and began to run for the bedroom.

"I told Albert I'd think about it," she yelled over her shoulder. "But I told him that you'd have to be very nice to me." Now she was running as fast as her high-heeled feet would take her. "And so far you haven't been!" She ran into the bedroom and slammed the door shut behind her, then braced it with her body.

"Lily, you're lying again," Trent bellowed through the door.

"All's fair," she retorted. "You haven't exactly been the soul of veracity yourself."

"What do you mean?"

"I mean that Albert's always known we weren't married. You told him. But you didn't tell me."

"He told you that?" Trent sounded shocked.

"Yes, he did."

"He wasn't supposed to. I made him promise."

"Well, maybe he feels a touch of loyalty to me. Maybe he thought it was just a little unfair to keep me in the dark. Maybe he thought that it was time to trick you. Now, how do you like it?"

There was no response.

"Trent?" Lily called. But he didn't answer.

She opened the door a crack, didn't see him, and then opened it all the way. He wasn't in the hallway. She went into the living room. He was sitting on the couch.

"I had it all planned," he said, chagrined.

Lily almost felt sorry for him, he looked so dejected.

"Some men," she began as she sat next to him, "when they want to marry a woman, just ask."

"You'd say no." He looked at her and his eyes were deep and soft. He had never looked more vulnerable. Her heart went out to him.

"Why don't you try?"

"You'll just tell me to go to hell," he said.

"Take a chance."

He turned to her and clasped her hands in his. "Will you marry me, Lily? Will you save me from a life of crime?"

That familiar tingling was beginning at the back of her neck.

"On your knees," she commanded haughtily, but she was grinning from ear to ear.

He knelt before her and repeated his question. "Will you marry me, Lily?"

"I think I might be able to see my way clear," she said imperiously.

"Say yes," he threatened.

"I'm not sure," she mumbled evasively. "I might have to consider it a bit further."

"Say yes, Lily." Now he was standing over her "Or I

swear, I'm going to have to take you over my knee and give you—"

"Since you put it that way, Trent, yes."

He clasped her in his arms. "I knew you'd come around eventually." His arms were strong and sure around her, and his heart beat companionably against her breast. "Truce?" He beamed down at her.

"Truce," she murmured against his strong chest.

"No more fights?" he asked.

"Trent, let's not expect the impossible," she answered wryly.

"If we do, I know how to stop them," he said. "That look" was beginning to shine in his eyes.

"Oh. How?" Lily asked.

"I'll show you," he said, and lifted her off her feet. He headed for the bedroom. Then he showed her. And it didn't take much convincing before she was sure that he was absolutely right.

Silhouette Desire

Now Available

Fabulous Beast by Stephanie James

Before, Tabitha had only studied the elusive
beasts of legend. Then she rescued Dev Colter
from danger on a remote island and
found that she had awakened a
slumbering dragon

Political Passions by Suzanne Michelle

Newly-elected mayor Wallis Carmichael was
furious to discover that sensual Sam Davenport
was really a Pulitzer Prize-winning journalist.
Politics and journalism don't mix—and now
she had to find out if he was just another
reporter out for a story.

Madison Avenue Marriage
by Cassandra Bishop

Famous mystery writer Lily Lansden needed a
"husband" for her winery commercial and
Trent Daily fitted the bill. But when the
game of pretend turned into real love could
Lily give up her Madison Avenue marriage?

Silhouette Desire

Now Available

Between the Covers by Laurien Blair

Everything changed between co-authors Adam and Haley when they began writing their ninth book together—a romance. Were they only playing out a story or were they friends now unleashing desires restrained for too long?

To Touch the Fire by Shirley Larson

Raine had loved Jade since she was sixteen—but he was her sister's husband. Now her sister had left him—would his bitterness and her guilt over the past threaten their awakening passions?

On Love's Own Terms by Cathlyn McCoy

Luke Ford had been out of Bonnie's life for seven years. But now her devastating husband wanted a second chance, and Bonnie's common sense was betrayed by a passion that still burned.

Silhouette Desire

Coming Next Month

Love And Old Lace by Nicole Monet

Burned once, Virginia had decided to swear off
romance and settle for a sensible, chaste
existence—but seductive Lucas Freeman
stormed her defences and neither her
body nor her heart could resist.

Wilderness Passion by Lindsay McKenna

Libby wanted to be ready for anything when she
met her unwilling partner on the environmental
expedition. But nothing prepared her for
Don Wagner, and the mountain trek suddenly
became a journey into a world of desire.

Table For Two by Josephine Charlton

Hadley and Lucas had shared a youthful love.
Now, when Hadley had landed in his embrace
once more, history repeated itself and left
them both determined that this time they
would not have to say goodbye.

Silhouette Desire

Coming Next Month

The Fires Within by Aimee Martel

As a female firefighter, Isabel was determined to be "one of the boys"—but no one made her feel more a woman than Lt. Mark Grady. Passion blazed between them, but could they be lovers *and* co-workers?

Tide's End by Erin Ross

Chemical engineer on an offshore oil rig, Holly had vowed never to engage in a "platform romance". Kirk's touch could make her forget her promises, but would his dangerous job as a diver keep them apart?

Lady Be Bad by Elaine Raco Chase

Though Noah had broken her heart six years before, Mariayna still loved him. Now she would attend his wedding with only one aim in mind—she would break all the rules to have him back again.

THE MORE SENSUAL
PROVOCATIVE ROMANCE

95p each

115 ☐ GAMBLER'S
WOMAN
Stephanie James

116 ☐ CONTROLLING
INTEREST
Janet Joyce

117 ☐ THIS BRIEF
INTERLUDE
Nora Powers

118 ☐ OUT OF
BOUNDS
Angel Milan

119 ☐ NIGHT WITH
A STRANGER
Nancy John

120 ☐ RECAPTURE
THE LOVE
Rita Clay

121 ☐ LATE RISING
MOON
Dixie Browning

122 ☐ WITHOUT
REGRETS
Brenda Trent

123 ☐ GYPSY
ENCHANTMENT
Laurie Paige

124 ☐ COLOUR MY
DREAMS
Edith St. George

125 ☐ PASSIONATE
AWAKENING
Gina Caimi

126 ☐ LEAVE ME
NEVER
Suzanne Carey

127 ☐ FABULOUS
BEAST
Stephanie James

128 ☐ POLITICAL
PASSIONS
Suzanne Michelle

129 ☐ MADISON
AVENUE
MARRIAGE
Cassandra Bishop

130 ☐ BETWEEN THE
COVERS
Laurien Blair

131 ☐ TO TOUCH
THE FIRE
Shirley Larson

132 ☐ ON LOVE'S
OWN TERMS
Cathlyn McCoy

All these books are available at your local bookshop or newsagent, or can be ordered direct from the publisher. Just tick the titles you want and fill in the form below.

Prices and availability subject to change without notice.

SILHOUETTE BOOKS, P.O. Box 11, Falmouth, Cornwall.

Please send cheque or postal order, and allow the following for postage and packing:

U.K. – 50p for one book, plus 20p for the second book, and 14p for each additional book ordered up to a £1.63 maximum.

B.F.P.O. and EIRE – 50p for the first book, plus 20p for the second book, and 14p per copy for the next 7 books, 8p per book thereafter.

OTHER OVERSEAS CUSTOMERS – 75p for the first book, plus 21p per copy for each additional book.

Name ....

Address ....

....